CW01083054

THE UNRAVELLING

A Futuristic Thriller of Technology and Betrayal in a World on the Brink of Collapse

By

Will Gibson

Grosvenor House
Publishing Limited

The right of Will Gibson to be identified as the author of this
work has been asserted in accordance with Section 78
of the Copyright, Designs and Patents Act 1988

The book cover is copyright to Will Gibson
Book cover art by Devon Mason

This book is published by
Grosvenor House Publishing Ltd
Link House
140 The Broadway, Tolworth, Surrey, KT6 7HT.
www.grosvenorhousepublishing.co.uk

A CIP record for this book
is available from the British Library

Paperback ISBN 978-1-80381-674-6
Hardback ISBN 978-1-80381-675-3
eBook ISBN 978-1-80381-676-0

Acknowledgements

For Elijah and Xanthe, for lighting up my life and keeping me moving forward. For Victoria, my soulmate, who makes everything possible.

Preface

In the year 2038, humanity stands on the edge of chaos, divided into two distinct realms: the pristine AI-governed suburbs, and the lawless urban wastelands beyond. As a disillusioned English boy hatches an audacious plan to save his beloved Asian pop star from the world's horrors, fate pulls a weary New York cop into the heart of an unfathomable global conspiracy.

Step into a world where the line between order and chaos is razor-thin, and the stability of civilisation teeters on the brink of collapse. When a wave of unprecedented system failures engulfs everything from driverless vehicles to the stock market, only one man, Joe Jones, can untangle the web of deceit and sabotage.

As he races against time to save his estranged family and the enigmatic pop star Suki, Joe faces the daunting task of uncovering the truth behind the mysterious British boy's actions, which threaten to unleash apocalyptic consequences. With the survival of humanity at stake, can Joe foil the sinister plot and prevent man's own creations from extinguishing the human race?

Dive into this gripping futuristic thriller where the fragility of human existence collides with the relentless advance of technology, and discover the lengths to which one man will go to protect the ones he loves and avert the annihilation of our world.

Contents

1 Happy Birthday

'Good morning, Joe.'

The whispering whirr of the motor is first, then the vertical movement of the blind reveals the shaft of light: wider, stronger. Consciousness begins, flickering eyes reveal the whitewashed ceiling.

'Today is Saturday, Joe. It's 06.45 and your coffee is waiting for you in the lounge machine. You have nine minutes to fully use the bathroom and get changed before it starts to go cold. Today's suggested outfit is on your wardrobe.'

Lifting his head slowly, he sees an image of himself where the mirror used to be. Also shorts, T-shirt, sneakers and socks. Another screen suddenly appears on the wardrobe door. *CNN* runs through the news while below, a list of daily tasks awaits completion. As he stirs, 'Wake Up' receives a green tick and disappears from the list.

'Today is Benji's birthday, Joe. I've prepped the card and the present, which you can collect in your Delivery Centre downstairs. You have 45 minutes before you'll be collected to visit him.

Benji is his six-year-old son—no, seven years old today. He is all attitude and intelligence beyond his years. Joe smiled at the thought of his gift: an old school remote-controlled car. It was not one of those ubiquitous GoogleCabs that would be coming to collect him soon, but a real mini racing car: hard lines, petrol, attitude, smoke. A German Audi rally car from the days before such pollutants were finally banned for good—when fun was allowed. Such a long time ago. He hadn't seen Benji for a couple of weeks now as his mother had taken him away on a short break. She swore it wasn't with Josh, her ex-boss and now her 'confidant'—like Joe knew what that meant! She'd been going crazy for ages—and so had Joe—her desire for calm and control and safety at real odds with the excitement that Joe sought from time to time, the adrenaline no longer available from his job—or from many parts of life now. He missed Benji. He was the reason he got up in the morning. He had high hopes for the kid. He was a clever little dude, remembering all the flags of the world at four years old, and most of the capital cities of the world too, with both his parents being slightly taken aback by his slightly eidetic memory. They bonded over sports and computers, as most dads did with their sons, yet Joe despaired at the shield around kids these days, he being of the generation that had been born in the late 1900s – late '90s to be precise. He had been able to travel freely, to shoot a gun—heck to *own* a gun— and to mix with other people who were different, in the days before people went slightly mad in the early '20s with the sudden and dramatic rise of hard liberalism all over the planet. His father was an old-fashioned cowboy type—well an urban cowboy from Brooklyn—but he loved cars and bars and was a real man's man. Joe would often join him in his garage, and tinkered with cars in the early 2000s, revelling in the company of the other guys who would be so cutting with him, sometimes even cruel, as he was often sent on impossible errands and given "long stands" to the amusement of the rest of the crew. Nothing bad, mind you, and Joe reflected that it had built his character. He could talk to pretty much anyone of any background, and those social skills stood him in great stead during his education and early career as he really tried to make it as a cop with a badge, who could go even higher.

CNN showed the date and time on the screen where his outfit used to be:

06.46, Tuesday, September 21, 2038.

The constant movement of the screens and the yellow tickers provided a comforting glow at the start of the day, and Joe would always catch up with whatever was happening before doing anything else. Though today he didn't want to get caught up in his X app: that Elon Musk super-app that was part citizen's journalism, part news app, and part messaging app. He could get lost in that feed for hours, and it had enabled the mass convergence of mainstream media, if not the impartiality of it. At least it was possible to filter out the rubbish on the X app—the consensus opinion always being easy to find and often the closest thing to the truth—CNN being heavily sponsored by the Government, even though that was denied. It was always drip-feeding you the latest narrative and the Government's agenda of the day, or the hour. This was a fast-changing world indeed.

The cool of the real wooden floor on his bare feet was interrupted by the soft rug in front of his pristine white sofa in the spacious lounge. His apartment was minimal and unfussy, clean white lines giving way to glass and views across to Manhattan, intermittently interrupted by moving AutoCasts of the HIM, the voice, without whom it seemed no one could function anymore. Once they had cracked AI, the production of mass Autobots like the HIM hadn't taken long. These helpers made the three-day work week possible by planning every aspect of your life and work. The HIM was everywhere, seemingly one step ahead of your thoughts and your needs. Life was on autopilot.

Home Intelligence Master. It was supposed to have a name. You were supposed to rename it like you did way back when the same had happened with your wifi name. But hardly anyone bothered. Same now. The HIM ruled the house. Never mind, he made good coffee. He even reordered the milk when it ran low.

The sun was just coming up over the skyline, and the lack of clouds suggested the forthcoming day was going to be an unseasonably hot one. Though he couldn't quite see Central Park, there were a few trees here and there that clung on to their green coats, and the late September morning would start gloriously and then hopefully stay that way for the day.

'HIM, show me the Jets briefing from last night,' barked Joe as he settled back into his lounger, freshly brewed coffee already beginning to wake him further. And the myriad of screens around him flickered into life as he watched a training brief of his team before the big game on Sunday against the Dolphins. Sport had morphed over the years into being part reality show, part entertainment series, and every aspect of their regimes was filmed and broadcast live, or most likely, instantly, on demand catch up. It was all voice-activated; no remotes to find. The HIM would sort all that out. Since the media rights revolution in the late twenties, the NFL had broadcast its own entertainment, increasing image rights and TV revenues year on year, and it had maintained its standing as the most valuable sporting event in the world. Getting 24/7 access to practice drills, locker room chats, even one-on-one coach to player chats, had dumbed the content a little for some, with accusations of staging and scripting like the old WWE wrestling way back in the day.

Yawn.

At least there was something to do today, thought Joe to himself as he headed into his bathroom and stared at himself in the mirror while brushing his teeth. A yellow star appeared in the corner of the mirror with a loud 'ping!' followed by 'WELL DONE, JOE! +20 points' as he spat out the minty toothpaste and collected his health reward for a positive habit completed.

'Prep the shower, HIM. I'll have it 39°C today, please. Medium hard jets.' Buttons and levers still existed in some places, but the ubiquity of a system controlling and prepping your world was everywhere now—at least in the home. Even some of the older flats still had heavy home automation now, with a HIM in almost every property, learning your routine, encouraging you to live well, managing your calendar and attending to your every need.

He shot his pyjama shorts into the laundry vacuum, and the HIM acknowledged that a coloured run would soon be underway as the basket was full, and could he collect it fully dried later that evening and transfer it to the IroningBot. The screen in the right window sprang to life, blocking out the sunrise and displaying his task list for the day, this particular task being set for 18.30, seeing as Joe didn't even confirm or object. No objections meant the HIM knew best and it was in command. It would remind him later on in the day, and perhaps even nag him a little until he did it.

The feminine curves of the GoogleCab shot into view on the screen in the left window, the map then appearing and indicating it would arrive in the AutoDock in three minutes and forty seconds. Pulling on his sneakers and finishing the still warm dregs of his coffee, Joe left his apartment for his date with Benji.

It was, as predicted, a hot one, being 80+°F, or so he reckoned, so the cool flush of his pre-prepared 68°F air hit him like a spring breeze as he settled into his cab ride, his entertainment choices already loaded on the screen. The journey would take 47.5 minutes exactly, so his movie wish list was greyed out on the selection panel. Feeling nostalgic and optimistic, he opted for some early noughties rock and settled back into the chair. The car silently pulled away, save for a small growl—that fake noise to alert users and passengers alike that movement was beginning— one of those things that was put there during the mass shift to electric vehicles in the late twenties that had stayed out of habit even when it was not really needed anymore. Who exactly *walked* anywhere now? Certainly not in the burbs anyway.

A giant dashboard screen flashed a picture in front of his eyes: a woman, mid-30s, brown straight hair, beautiful. Monica.

'Morning.'

'Just checking to see you're on time, I don't have access to your GoogleCabs account now, so I can't—'

'Yes, yes, I haven't forgotten.' The irritation clearly audible in his voice. 'I said I'd be there for 08.00 and

I will. Don't worry, you'll make your whatever-it-is-that's-so-important.'

'Good.'

'Or *whoever*,' he muttered under his breath, which was clearly heard, but ignored.

Monica was Joe's first love, the mother of his child, but now estranged, lost to him because of those crazies at her office that were all evangelistic about philanthropy and changing the world, bottles of Evian stuck constantly up their arses as they exercised like mad and did all the 'right things'. They all sat like ancient hippies, singing happy-clappy songs such as 'Kum ba ya, my Lord'. All desperate to live longer, as if a century plus wasn't long enough in this boring shithole without at least trying to *live* life. It was Benji who brought out their differences, Monica being the safety blanket. She insisted on one of those MyHealth bands that reminded you every time your water level was below optimum that you should drink. It even suggested your next meal so your pH and minerals could be balanced to promote optimum cell growth.

Joe wanted to have fun! Like playing baseball outdoors for once instead of in a hermetically sealed astrodome where the temperature and moisture levels were controlled; where the air was pumped with chemicals to ensure no one caught a cold from anyone else; where the food was so bland and unappealing as it matched to your HealthBand. Live, live, live seemed to be the motto for the masses now—except they weren't living. They were merely *existing*. The average age of the middle classes was well over 100 now, and the burden of cost on all states worldwide to care for the ageing population had changed the dynamics of the world.

Joe had seen the ugly side of that, being a public order facilitator—or cop, in old speak— as he'd been to the hoods, the shanties, during his training. He'd wanted to be a Level 1, a member of the elite, one of those who actually shot and fought with the bad guys, the ones who had danger. That was the thrilling part, the part that made him feel *alive*. Except his knee had had other ideas, and despite a bionic transplant, it was forbidden to be a Level 1 without being a million per cent healthy. Evian up the arse indeed!

So his life was a Level 3 in the Sleeping Zones— suburbia, if you will—where his mandate was to watch and observe, answer questions and mostly direct people back into their automated lives. The greatest excitement came from people asking their GCabs to wait too long for them in an undesignated spot. A quick chat with the car and a call through to the customer's rig was usually enough to move it on back to the vast parking lots where thousands upon thousands of cars all waited for their next instruction or next call. Littering the streets with parked cars was a complete no-no, but if you were lucky, you could pay a premium for one of the old, real customer car parking spaces in front of the parade of shops. Only mostly there weren't many shops anymore, save for a few experiential showrooms where the newest and latest gadgets could be displayed. Shops still existed in the town and city centres, the lawless places that he wasn't allowed to go into. That was for the Level 2 and Level 1 guys only, and usually only nightshifts at that.

People in the cities were mainly left to their own devices. They had shops alright, old-fashioned retail units which were stocked on a day-to-day basis with things people needed and wanted. Alcohol, meds, all sorts of smoking devices, including maybe—if you could afford it—some of the real good stuff: paper-covered smokes, real ones like in the old days before they were all strictly controlled like everything else nowadays. You could get some beers still, but only a limited quantity at a time, and as for anything harder, forget it. Controlled. You could only drink in certain places. Restaurants were still a big thing for those who had prosperity and loved to socialise and show themselves off. While they could get smashed on wine and cognac and whatever else took their fancy inside the restaurant, they had to extend their stay with time in a Hydration Station, a recovery pod, so to speak. Before they left, the toxins were flushed and salts and fluids replaced to remove the 'danger' before catching their pre-ordered GoogleCabs back to their own places. It took about 30 minutes, and all restaurants had at least 20 or so, all of them being heavily subsidised by the Government—once they did eventually bring limits in on the alcohol. Petty squabbles and fights would often ensue if you missed your slot and then the whole group had to wait longer while you detoxed. If you tried to skip it, the GCab wouldn't work. And even if you lived nearby and walked home and you were stopped by a trooper of any sort—even a bored Level 3 cop like Joe—you'd pay for it big time.

Huge swathes of the population were teetotal now anyway, with anything that was 'proven' to limit life expectancy being effectively shunned or labelled as disgusting behaviour, just like the vegan and don't-eat-animals stuff way back in the early twenties. It all started in the schools and universities with hard left doctrine now being a way of the world. And anyone who didn't like it, or who dared to speak up, was a social outcast, a pariah. You had better do what you were told, else you were a 'bad person'.

His mind was drifting through his everyday: the sunshine, the endless GoogleCabs, the soft whirr of the GrassBots as they kept the world so neat and tidy. It just, well, worked... I mean, working the mandatory three-day week, introduced a few years before so that more people could have jobs, so that they didn't go stir crazy from cabin fever and raise the suicide rate any higher, wasn't so bad. He saw his buddies from time to time but always in one of those SafeBars where you had five hours to go crazy and drink beers and shots to your heart's content, with music as live you were gonna get these days, all from vending machines, video walls and the HIM helping your playlists, before your time ran out and you had to recuperate in the recovery pod. Alcohol was strictly controlled out in the burbs, and the authorities wouldn't let anyone go over their safe limits, so only two options: go off the grid in the hoods where very little could be controlled—dangerous—or hit up in the SafeBars or a restaurant where you could have a medically treated blowout and be sure of your safety.

The sun shone overhead, glistening on the grass as a baby rolled over from a sitting position onto his front. Eyes on the prize, the picnic basket lay a metre or so away, a long way for those little arms, but determined as he was, the little boy made his way towards it. Determination in his eyes, he inched forward in a classic crawl motion. The blonde lady stood up quickly, adjusting her head downwards in a ducking motion as she set the plane of her recording device in motion, the rim of her GGlasses moving towards horizontal so she could get the best shot of this moment.

'Look at him go!' roared the man relaxing on the other side of the basket, cold beer in hand, obviously one of his quota for that week. He smiled and surveyed the perfect scene in front of him. Just as the child made to grab the basket, his hand was whipped away by the fast-moving lady as she scooped the baby up in one arm and did a kind of barrel roll to avoid collision with the picnic lunch.

'Easy tiger, not your lunch!' she said as she collapsed in a fit of giggles near the smiling man. Joe smiled as he surveyed the perfect family scene, pangs of guilt hitting his stomach as he realised what he didn't have anymore, and why. Fuck them! The happy-clappy shits. The fucking hard left Liberals, who pretended to be saving the world when really it was just a fucking ruse to allow the politicians to control every whim of their lives and get richer. Except the sheep couldn't comprehend that. No way was the amazing President Obama II anything more than a philanthropic angel sent to this world to help the USA stay the most important nation on earth. She and her late husband had devoted their lives to this great nation and no, she wouldn't dream of squirrelling away millions and billions of ill-gotten gains from supporters and other governments alike. No way.

Kings of Leon moved onto their next guitar-driven anthem, rasping vocals and melodies filling the car in contrast to the sunlight outside and the cool 68° inside. The windows were dimming just enough to remove the glare but still enabling Joe, now he'd fully woken, to see the all-green manicured verges as he was taken towards his son.

It took him a while to recognise the pain. It had been so long since anything had intruded on his world that it took even longer to recognise the dizziness and the crushing bang that produced the warm sticky flow from his nose: blood covering the soft beige seat cushions of his cab.

There wasn't much noise, save for a hissing outside and some smoke. Then, wiping the blood away to stop it from trickling into his mouth, he saw the scene outside. The crash. The impossible.

2 The Book

Needles. Condoms. Rats.

He stepped over the putrid pavement, the mizzle following him like a state trooper clings to a drug boy. Giant OLED screens were seemingly watching his every move as they advertised their wares, from beer to God to girls and everything in between. An all-night porno house was still going, hardcore nonsense streaming from the noise leaking from its old underground street cellar. The muscled black stud gave it good and proper to the pneumatic blonde. Both were looking as bored as they were dead behind the eyes, unlike the Asian grandfather peering over the stage for a better view, like one of those old Mr Chip cartoon heads.

He wasn't far from home now, but he'd still have to be careful, and his plan meant that a cop stop could be catastrophic, especially if they found his prize, and what was in The Book. He was desperate to look at it but couldn't risk the rain ruining it. His eyes were failing in the night to reveal the detail of what was in it. He was so distracted by the contents that he switched off, and was nervous of being jumped—or worse, stopped by the night troopers.

05.00. Light was starting to peel through the safe black curtains of night as he skipped over another pile of fetid kerb-shit. Up to the other side of the road, instinctively he moved out of sight, hitting a doorway as he thought he heard the whirr of a trooper's bike. Pressing himself as close to the door as he could and turning his eyes into the damp brick so the sensors couldn't find his eyes, he cursed his stupid judgement for being out after curfew, for possibly being caught so close to his mission taking off.

The oversized front wheel squidged and slushed as it threw up raindrops and sludge from the street. The exaggerated dome in the middle of the bike housed the trooper, his blue scanner treading the forward path, slightly side by side as it peeked onto both pavements. If he clung tightly to the door, as long as his breath or his eyes didn't wander into the beam, he'd be fine, and hopefully it would pass.

Not that it was a crime per se to be out after 02.00, but it meant an automatic stop if you were caught in any one of the seven or eight Night Time Boroughs that made up the Central and East End of London. From Soho to Covent Garden and on through the City towards East Ham, these were the wastelands of London, which were lawless in the day when the sheer weight of population meant that trying to keep control was pointless. Rather than the Government giving away total control, they heavily policed the night, reckoning that nothing good came after 02.00, and if you were a normal citizen, you'd *want* to be at home plugged into your Hydration Station, watching movies or TV serials, or at the very least running around Virtual Town with your mates, racking up pointless VR points, which you could redeem for grocery store coupons.

The trooper bike was the other side of him now, its rear sensor giving a less concentrated field of view but wider, so he clung even tighter to the brick and the door, and waited. His hand reached around inside his overcoat, the crisp leather edges of his prize keeping him occupied, a sense of nervous anticipation adding to his heightened senses. He was mentally in two places at once. Here, now. Cold and damp. Afraid and watching. And there, home: opening his highly sought-after bounded diary, eagerly lifting the algorithms, and the code to input as part of his plan.

The trooper bike turned the corner, and in a flash, Dylan was gone, skipping back along the pavement, this time with more purpose, annoyed by his near miss, and determined to get back and survey his plan. The meeting had gone well. He'd worried about The Book being stolen right back as soon as he'd handed over the cash, but the source was good. His instinct told him that the motivation for sale was quick and easy cash for drugs, despite the sharp suit and the eau-de-banker aura that surrounded him. Something told Dylan that this guy didn't care what he was going to do with the info. He only cared about his next fix. And he was probably right.

He knew the back way through the old multi-storey. Once a prime piece of real estate but now mostly deserted, this part of town was not safe enough to be a halfway house for the GCabs, and no one was spending millions on city centre real estate now anyway. They had long killed off the concept of the office since the Covid debacle of the early twenties. Working from home had thrown real estate markets into a spin all over the world as the traditional concept of the city centre died out as a form of housing big business. Elon Musk was the first to rebel, moving his entire HQ of the X-App out of downtown San Francisco in 2025—or sometime around then—after one of his VPs was stabbed to death in broad daylight while popping out for lunch. It was around this time, but it happened slowly, that cities themselves ceased to become important anywhere. The lack of daytime Monday–Friday economy had crippled the value of the space. Commercial rents had nosedived and nearly everyone worked from home, until even that was stopped. It began being controlled in the early thirties with the setup of the suburban offices, often taking the place of large supermarkets or hyperstores that had also mostly long gone as everyone had their every need delivered by drone right to their doorstep.

Retailers now were nothing of the sort you would remember, and online e-commerce had exploded in the late twenties once they'd figured out the rules of the skies and how AI could control the buzz of the traffic above, as the drones delivered your every whim, sometimes two, three or four at a time, depending on what you were ordering. Retail companies themselves had morphed almost into marketing agencies with carefully curated lists and categories of goods well organised so you could find what you needed. And the AR capability of the GGlasses enabled you to 'see' whatever it was you wanted to buy, with sumptuous fresh fruit displays being particularly inviting on the eyes. Nearly everyone had a rig, as they were sometimes called, the glasses being connected to the HIM that controlled your world 24/7. That could order ahead for you, make a call, take a photo or capture some video right from your glasses. The Chinese had experimented in the mid-thirties with the first implant, but the West was as ever highly sceptical of anything China did and would not sign off the technology for use in the States or in Europe. Many did so on the black market and even tried to disguise that they'd had it by wearing a pair of glasses so they didn't stand out.

Fingerprints to the dash, eyes close to the scanner, Dylan hurried into the foyer of his building and towards the lift he'd taken thousands of times. Calling it, he hit floor 10 and then jumped straight back out, scooting along the side wall towards the back of the building. What if he'd been followed? They'd be checking the lift, so his little double back was his clever yet rudimentary way to protect himself. Watching. Waiting.

Nothing.

He called the lift again, and this time his correct floor 12 gave access to his door. After a thorough inspection of the frame, he was in. And four locks later, he felt safe. Time for The Book.

'Where have you *been* at this time of night?' said the shrill, yet whispered, voice from the corner of the living room.

'Don't worry. It's nothing, Mama, just an errand,' he said as he made for his bedroom, swinging his arms sharply behind his shoulders in an attempt to hide The Book.

Once inside, and with no further admonishment from the other side of the door, his gaze fell back to The Book. Turning the pages gingerly he could see the code, he could see the system architecture diagrams, and he smiled.

Dylan had been learning to code ever since he was a kid. Ever since the AI Wars of the mid-twenties, it was clear that you had to be able to 'do' things in this world or you would never get out of the inner-city shit. You had to either manage the people who did things, which was never going to happen to a kid from the wrong side of the tracks, or you had to be able to create, to code, to manage the plethora of machines and systems that made our world happen. If you could get machine A to talk to machine B and issue an instruction that could be understood and an action carried out as a result, then you were valuable in this world. It was the way towards riches for Dylan, and getting his hands on The Book was another part of his plan so that he could understand what really went on deep in the backends of the AI systems and in the very secretive world of Google, and of Alphabet.

It was 05.30 now and Dylan knew he had to get some sleep, as tomorrow would be a busy day. He'd seen enough in The Book to know it was exactly what he wanted and needed to know, and he crawled into his bed, satisfied with his adventure.

It was quite a while before morning squeezed sufficiently underneath the blinds and he woke ever so gently and tried to appear normal. Keeping his routine the same, he did little to arouse suspicion—as if it mattered in his mother's apartment—for what he was about to try, to test, would be the culmination of his intellect, his coming of age, proof that he was indeed a giant among lesser mortals. He should be revered.

'What time do you call this, Dylan? What have I told you about sneaking around at night and being on your computers at all hours?'

He ignored his mother and headed for the fridge. Orange juice, that would do.

Gulping down the sweet juice right from the carton, he knew he risked his mother's ire once more with such uncouth habits. He could easily get a glass, but he didn't care as after today, he would be gone anyway, and she would no longer matter.

'It's OK, Mum, I'm actually doing a really vital research assignment, and I'm getting paid to code something really cool for this company. I'll get some cash later today if it goes well.'

'OK, whatever. Good. We need some. Look, I'm going to be late for work, I'll see you later, OK?'

She moved towards him for a kiss goodbye on the head, but he stayed in character and swerved her advance at the last minute, giving her a rare smile as he tiptoed back to his room.

Hearing the door shut with a bang, he wasted no time in finding what he was looking for. A pneumatic blonde appeared on stage at what appeared to be a live concert. The camera panned and swerved as her silver dress always stayed central in the view, but the footage appeared to constantly switch between first-person view, overhead drone shots and professionally shot footage of the concert. She roared into her first song:

'Dreamer. You are all I need, all I want, all I neeeeeeeedddd...'

Tapping more keys, the scene shifted now to what appeared to be a hotel corridor. Back to first person, the blonde was still there, gesturing to the viewer and asking for a hand as she opened the door to a penthouse suite.

Once inside, she beckoned suggestively to the bedroom and the camera of course followed as she reached behind her neck to unfasten something. Then she flicked the corner of her dress off with her right arm, performing a shimmy first with her shoulders and then her hips as the dress fell to the floor. She was a picture of beauty. She must have been five feet six tall at the most, and wow, what a body! So natural. Legs to die for, seductive hips and breasts that didn't move an inch as she reached behind her again and unclasped her bra, which also fell to the floor.

She advanced towards the camera now, dropping to her knees and looking up at the lens, smiling seductively again, as the sound of the zip was unmistakable. Dylan was a young man clearly with needs, and his were going to be met right now as he snuggled back under the covers of his bed.

A few hours later, he awoke refreshed, and got to work. Checking the time, he needed to complete his tasks before 16.00, his time, ready for his plan, well, the *test* of his plan to see if everything else was able to be put in motion.

Dylan was in high-energy mode now, his frantic bashing of the keys only matched by the movements of his head between keyboard and book, back to book, back to keyboard, and only occasionally up at the screens.

'Creating digital cousin. Please wait…'

He waited.

His processing power was up against it, but he was harnessing other fire power in the cloud, so he knew it would take a while. He just had to be patient.

An hour went by in what seemed like minutes.

Tapping his system awake, he fingered the keys feverishly, as if performing a frantic piano solo from back in the day. *That guy with the stupid colourful suits, what was his name? Ah, never mind.* Keys rattling, all the while looking back and forward at The Book, occasionally stopping to digest the next layer of system architecture until the money shot was revealed, the main event. And there was silence! Had he done it? Switching screens, he saw the sunshine, the camera view from on high, the GoogleCab, the intersection, the traffic lights. The crash. And he smiled.

3 RO707

'Drast-voot-yie.'

General Adams rose, greeted by the delegation one by one: first the interpreter, then the boss, and then in turn, the entourage, the group of flunkies who did little except be there to give the boss an inflated sense of importance.

He knew the routine well, having been to Moscow many times when it was a fine upstanding city, when Russia was *the* powerhouse. This was also long before the final overthrow of Putin and the supposed World War Three of 2030, that wasn't really because the long-suffering Russian people made it very easy for the US and NATO forces to 'do the deed'. Like bin Laden and Hussein, Putin had been overthrown, 'terminated', but not before he'd gone totally cuckoo over the Orange Uprising in Ukraine, and the 'eternal war' that had started there in 2022. It had been Tymoshenko — not the actor turned puppet Zelenskyy—that finally did it.

She took charge in the late twenties once the West had had enough of Zelenskyy and his money laundering and the scandal that would have finally taken down Sleepy Joe if he hadn't died suddenly just as the news broke about exactly how they had been passing money back and forth between the US and Ukraine. Zelenskyy got what was coming to him alright and was looking at jail for the rest of his days, even if Biden wasn't there to face the music with him.

Once Tymoshenko agreed to take charge once again, she galvanised Ukraine and took out the neo-Nazis who had been hiding under the Zelenskyy regime. This allowed a clear focus on defeating Putin, and after almost a decade of raiding the public purse to keep paying for endless more tanks and weapons, Putin finally went too far by ordering another jet to be taken down.

Still glamorous and all-blonde cornrows in the autumn of her life, Tymoshenko staged her hunger strike that finally united the Ukrainian people—once she'd figured out how harnessing social media—and *CNN*—could get her the groundswell of public opinion that she eventually got. It's one thing seeing your babushka in pain, but it was another seeing the Princess Leia-like Tymoshenko, almost 78 years young, oozing sense as she proved the atrocities of Putin in Crimea were real. The final straw was the series of downed jet liners between 2018 and 2029 that got the international community up in arms when she presented the truth to the world, live on Global TV on that fateful Saturday morning... Putin fired on Berlin this time as there was nothing really left in Kyiv anyway. This meant devastation to millions, but by then the international community would stand it no more. Emboldened by the complete standstill of Moscow for two long winter months, with army defections crippling the State's ability to control, Putin was finally captured in a daring Kremlin raid, freeing the East and heralding a new age of democracy in Russia and the old CIS states.

The room was old-fashioned and mahogany, save for the myriad of screens, cameras and microphones, which had everything spoken simultaneously picked up, recorded and translated back for the watching teams on both sides. Adams imagined that it must have always been like this, save for the New Age tech, and that the culture of the Russians really had been preserved. Rare these days, as he thought of the ubiquity of the USA culture which, despite a hundred and more years of racial tolerance, was still more or less split into white and black, albeit with some crossover. *Some things never change*, he thought.

The rare late September snow began to fall again on the city, which was already covered in a beautiful powder-like brightness that cheered up the dull granite and steel. It looked like extremely expensive make-up which had been gingerly applied on the face of the most beautiful lady in a way that only master artists can do. Except this was real. It was nature. This was snow.

Taking his seat for the presentation, he noticed the distinct lack of GGlasses on the attendees. He reflected on the elongated nature of the double *G*, which almost made any speaker of the word sound as if they had a stutter when they pronounced the now infamous name of *the* tool from those masters-of-everything, Google. Not content with cars, cabs and the total domination of both wireless data *and* wireless power charging, the renamed GoogleGlasses had become omnipresent—particularly since the partnership with Apple to integrate the HIM in most markets.

Studying the Russians, he noticed their eyes were all over the place and it clicked. They'd all had the implant. Banned in the US owing to the risk of brain swellings, aneurisms and eye strain, the WHO had rebelled against the Chinese-led invention that 'was going to change the world'. However, the Western vloggers that got access all had conspiracy theories of their own. These were mainly around IP security protocols that the West weren't going to allow into Chinese hands, even for only $5,000 a pop, which included the one-hour cyber-injection and modding process that it took to access your neurons. It was rumoured that the finest tech minds in the US were joining forces to come up with their own implant. However, nothing was public beyond the rumour phase as of yet.

A soft female voice spoke up from the screens:

> 'Gentlemen, prepare to meet the future of law enforcement, of border control and of... population control. Meet RO707, RealOffice 7version7.'

Soft applause accompanied the entrance of the robot gliding silently into the front of the room, a far cry from the eighties imagination of RoboCop and the noughties Japanese androids. This was majestic!

The metal trooper was at least six foot eight inches, and could have easily passed for playing basketball in the NBA. Though clad entirely in metal, it did not look totally solid, the sheen of the metallic panels almost appearing like skin, as if it could bend and move and breathe like real skin and muscles. There was indeed flex in a lot of the units, and you could see the curvature of the panels move just like a real leg muscle would. Clamped to its right ankle was a pistol, and on its left side an automatic rifle. The trooper had a skull-like shape for its head, and with eyes and nose and mouth, it tried to look as human as possible, save for one eye looking like a camera lens, as it was clearly super-charged and prioritised over the other one. On its back was slung a backpack of questionable material, part metal, part hard-wearing flex material, and it clearly contained extra ammo for the various weapons it had on display.

The screens either side of the bot lit up, one showing the first-person view that the robot could see with a clear heads-up display for everyone in front of it, and (United States CentralCo) tags giving the name. With a slight tilt of the head, the bot zoomed into Adams and brought up more data about the known subject.

'General James Adams, General US Central Command, 4 Star General CENTCOM [United States Central Command]' flashed the text beneath the live image of Adams sitting in his chair. 'Friendly,' continued the description as the bot walked half a step towards Adams and gave him a formal salute.

'At ease, solider,' replied Adams with a smile, as the attractive blonde to his right stood to take up the story.

'Please allow me to introduce myself. I am Marsha Robinson, Chief of Staff of the United States Central Command.'

She started slowly, aware that the translation bots were effectively doubling the amount of time it took her to present. She, in effect, had to speak twice as slowly, which was difficult, but she could compensate for this by introducing large pauses at the end of sentences—like uncomfortably large pauses.

'The RO707 is a fully configurable humanoid-style Autobot. Fully controllable with a series of AI interfaces which can instruct the trooper to carry out any assignment of your choice. Examples include standard policing to full-on military combat and attack bot. In addition, its AI capability and multi-channel comms frequencies mean it can communicate independently with other troopers deployed. This works if they have slightly different orders or even ranks assigned within a smaller unit.'

Robinson was flying now, and she enjoyed having her own voice rather than just being the go-to for Adam's every whim—as if automation itself couldn't sort everything he wanted anyway—but he still needed a human in the chain of command to make things efficient. Oh well, another year or so and she was convinced she'd have her promotion in the bag, especially if she nailed this deal with the decision makers in front of her. It was certainly going well so far, and the only two barriers to this huge deal going ahead were a lower cost pitch from the Chinese with an inferior product, or the shifting sands of moving budgets if one of the top brass over there decided to invest in other areas.

The deal was strategic for Adams, his being the chair of everything central in the US military, and this was his route towards that elusive fifth star. Establishing grade one US infrastructure on a vast landmass that bordered Europe, the Middle East, China itself and the Far East into Japan would be a huge boost for US Intelligence Services and would further cement the growing relationship between the old Russians and NATO that less than a decade ago had seemed impossible.

Robinson continued, and got to the point:

'The shelf life of each trooper is approximately 20 years, with a standard service interval every year, or every three months of active military deployment. That gives it ten times a return of the investment versus very fragile human capital doing the same roles when salaries, healthcare and other human benefits are compared like for like regarding the cost of the unit, servicing and the managed AI service that we automatically bundle with the units.'

Pause.

'I think you will find that this can solve all of your problems right now: racial integrations in Moscow, Saint Petersburg, Rostov and Volgograd. Remote border control all along the Siberian border with Mongolia and China. Active military combat in the Far East combatting the Asian drug smugglers coming in via Yakutsk and Vladivostok.'

Longer pause as she let that sink in.

'Quite frankly, ladies and gentlemen, our only competition is the Chinese bio-dog, Geda mark VIII. And while they perform admirably in unusual weather-related conditions, they are unsuitable for urban law and order. They perform poorly when faced with active combat situations in chasing down drug runners. And with a service interval that is almost four times the load, not to mention various public malfunctions, we firmly believe that this partnership and our proposal will help you achieve your objectives in the next decade and well into the fifties.'

A broad smile flashed across the face of General Adams as he reckoned the purchase order from the NRRF—the

New Republic of the Russian Federation—was in the bag. Not that they had much get-out due to their strong directives from NATO since the Putin overthrow, coupled with the global economic sanctions in place to prop the country up. The NRRF was a real hybrid now, a mix of the strong Russian culture, but softer, as though they were all so apologetic about getting Putin so wrong, a bit like Germany post-Hitler. The mass influx of immigration had done little to the peace ambitions of the new state—as lawlessness, gangs and racial tension were at an all-time high—but at least the new faces from Africa, Asia and the Middle East had given the place fresh impetus, and stimulated the decimated economy. Hence the need for the RO707s. Programmed to be impartial despite race or colour, it was felt that a core of bots in the police would lead to a more peaceful street... as well as propping up the military in the Far East where stopping the flow of drugs entering the land mass was proving to be a gigantic headache.

So, it was a done deal. With handshakes and nods, the agreement was for 15,000 units over three years, first to be deployed in Moscow then spreading to the other cities as discussed. The eastern frontier with the highest crime rate being the easiest smuggling route into the land mass from Japan and China, was in desperate need of reinforcements to combat the global drug epidemic. If boredom and a three-day week in the US had pushed up the suicide rate, then the drugs issue in the East was doing likewise in the 'other world'.

Leaving the beautifully preserved building 5 of the Kremlin, Adams beckoned to his team to follow.

'Where are we going, chief?' asked Robinson very cheerfully, almost too informally.

'For a walk. Can't come all this way and not *see* the city. Our hotel is only a block away.'

Cue nervous intercom shuffling from the security guys and cars moving around like a block party trying to organise parking for the neighbourhood. Crossing the cobbles of Red Square, past Lenin's mausoleum and GUM, the department store, Adams revelled in the unusually cold air of late September, the soft covering of white gently melting underfoot as he headed towards the intersection. Old technology interspersed with new juxtaposed against the giant sky screens along the commerce street of Tverskaya, and he wondered how old the traffic lights really were. Pulling on his GGlasses, the Cyrillic gave way to English, and he understood the lunch offer was ravioli from the faux Italian restaurant chain.

Some giant apparel flagship stores were intermingled with restaurants and offices along this very grand street, the ancient red bricks juxtaposed with the street screens that seemed to be everywhere now. Hanging from the top of buildings, angled down towards the citizens, you only saw them on the important streets, the ones where people would actually be, now that in-person activity was limited to certain parts of certain towns. Working in conjunction with your rig, adverts would shuck and jive and move 'at' you, coming to life when you'd least expect it, such as the restaurant chain sending down a giant piece of ravioli towards you on a fork. At least you could turn off the AR elements if you were that way inclined, but amazingly a high percentage of people did not. That's what the marketers claimed anyway.

An almighty sound shook the city. A boom and a bang, followed quickly by water everywhere, running so hard it was like a riot control cannon against the shoulders and chest. Security guys scrambled to surround Adams as they bundled him over the crossing and towards The Ritz. Such a force of nature. Real. Not a bomb. Not an act of terrorism. But monsoon rain in September? In Moscow? How had the temperature suddenly lifted like that? And rain this hard wasn't right, wasn't real. Something was wrong. Bursting through the Old-World revolving doors of the grand interior, the security entourage bundled Adams into the side conference room.

'OUT!' screamed the lead guard as a group of businessmen bolted for the door, bemused.

One of the guards shouted for the HIM to show the latest live Moscow news, and *Rossiya Today* instantly appeared on the huge screen to the centre of the boardroom. Live cameras in Moscow showed the city being hit by what was being called 'a storm of Biblical proportions', before it cut again to Sydney, where the same was happening.

4 Singapore Nights

Tall, tall buildings. Glass. Lights. Water. The view from her booth was unreal 71 floors up in The Stamford hotel. On the table was an eclectic mix of cocktails, all dry ice, real ice and colour, twinkling against the Singapore night sky.

The music was certainly New Age. A mix of low male voices rapping and every so often a distinct female melody ripping through the beats. Not a hit but something so achingly cool it couldn't possibly have been a commercial success. Not quite loud enough to drown out any conversation. You didn't have to shout to be heard, but maybe at certain parts of the song you had to raise your voice just a little.

Over near the bar, in one of the angular corners of the building's glass façade, Suki saw a big group of fans dancing, some of them wearing Suki T-shirts and some of them with silver glitter dresses, which was her trademark. No one bothered her, the VIP area being slightly quieter still. But the four gruff guards at all angles of the ropes had seen off enough autograph hunters for them to know they weren't getting near anyway, even if they tried. The tall thin girl in one of the silver dresses was the most intriguing, and Suki figured she–he was also a switcher, as the short black crop wouldn't have looked out of place on one of the guards. The military boots wouldn't have either, yet the mix of feminine make-up applied to one half of the face and a masculine tone on the other half, complete with black lips and eyes, was a mesmerising site. They—She? He? —could dance alright, and that was adding to the mood that Suki found herself pre-show, with some nerves flying through her system for sure.

She was pensive.

'What's up, Suki? Surely by now you aren't nervous?'

She jolted a little, as if being awoken from her spell, the comforting voice of her fiancé, who was half worried, half joking. 'No, I'm fine, honey, it's just… this view…'

The view was indeed one of the best anywhere in the world. The majesty of the Marina Bay in Singapore was well known for the colonial excellence of The Fullerton on the corner of the Bay next to the bridge, which still hosted the Grand Prix. Into the Bay itself and there was the still magnificent boat atop the cricket stumps of the Marina Bay Sands hotel and the twinkling light show that lit up the flower that is the ArtScience museum. This was indeed one of the greatest views anyone could witness anywhere.

Kelly was nonplussed. 'But surely it's a lot like Tokyo?' he said.

Kelly was her boyfriend of two years now, at first a hugely kept secret to ensure her share of the global music industry stayed, well, massive, but of course Suki's adoring fans *had* found out about her dalliance with a man. Recently, it had been carefully stage managed. It was known that she had a close male 'friend', but no one knew about the engagement. Maybe this is why she was so nervous, as that night's gig at the Singapore National Stadium was being broadcast around the world, and it had been decided to release the news live on stage.

'No, no, it's just this *view*! It's very different to Tokyo. The water and the criss-crossing roads and the mix of the small and the tall... It's lovely. I love coming to Singapore. I'm so lucky—lucky to have you,' she said, inching right into his side and nuzzling his neck.

Suki was a global phenomenon, the first Asian megastar that had cracked the West. In part, this was due to her untypical Asian hair, her blonde being very familiar to a Western audience. That along with the androgynous soft face and the impossible figure to die for. Her career had been one long lesson in marketing prowess with a series of raunchy YouTube videos going viral and grasping attention globally before a megadeal with Apple comprising songs, TV shows, cartoons and live gigs catapulted her into the forefront of global style. Her safe features and almost un-Japanese appearance, coupled with a hint of Asian accent, and a broad-brush appeal to the masses, had made her the biggest star around. Guys wanted to *be* with her. Girls wanted to *be* her. Mums loved her intelligence and New World attitude to lifestyle and fitness, and dads lusted over the impossible figure and the carefully hidden innuendos that smattered her work occasionally to draw the guys even further in.

'Hey, play *CNN*, at the screen near table 17,' interrupted Bob, the tour manager.

'You are both gonna want to see this...'

Suki's face appeared right in the middle of the maelstrom of graphics and texts, the yellow ticker and the constant position of the red and white logo a familiar sight. And her stomach dropped as she took in what was being shown and said:

> 'Speculation is just reaching us at *CNN* that Suki Yakamoto, The Asian Princess, is preparing to end her career of live touring around the world. She is due on stage at the National Stadium in Singapore tonight for another one of her sell-out gigs, and we are hearing that she will use the show to announce her closely guarded secret.'

> 'Yes, that's right, Lisa,' chimed in the other talking head as they continued, while Suki and her guests were silent and dumb-struck, and left staring at the giant screen in front of them.

> 'And her secret is? She's finally got a boyfriend!'

> 'Or perhaps a girlfriend, right, Steve?'

'Yes, that's right, Lisa. The identity of this mystery beau is none other than famous YouTuber and Insta influencer, Kelly Pieterson, who, as well as being famous for his love of fast cars, cocktails and the insane social media pranks that made him millions, is also one of the pioneers of the gender switching movement.'

'Yes, Steve, though the details here are sketchy. Born biologically male, Kelly first switched gender aged six years old when he transitioned to be a little girl and took on the name Kelly. He then transitioned back to male, aged 16, just as his social media career took off, and he is said to have inspired a generation of switchers who like to change their physical gender as dictated by their mental health.'

'Expensive business that, Steve, huh?' guffawed Lisa as she looked hard right to her fellow host and allowed him the floor once again.

Suki held her head in her hands and started scanning the table for indications as to who might have made this public. Someone had leaked this, but who? She ran to the rest room while the talking heads continued the story.

'Yes, Lisa, he famously had a relationship with fellow tuber Dave Huntsman—the one who does those NFL player skits online—while he was still male, aged 20, and then transitioned back to female while still dating

Dave. However, they did split up a year or so later. His social media career then went into overdrive as he became known for make-up techniques for gender-fluid humans, and he transitioned back to being physically male in 2034. He's certainly never mentioned Suki in any of his posts or on his channels, and this is a hugely kept secret that no doubt will be the talk of the town for weeks to come!'

'Switch that off, HIM!' barked Suki as she returned to the table and slumped in the corner, Kelly shuffling his backside along the suede-backed banquette to be next to her.

'Hey, come on, babe, that's *insane* publicity. *CNN* at prime time? We are going to be massive together, darling. Massive,' chirped an anxious but excited Kelly as he was actually relieved that their secret was finally out.

Suki rolled her eyes, and softly murmured, 'But this is not what we are doing this for, Kelly. We want privacy. A life. Anyway, I can't think about this now, I have to get my head space into the show.'

Her show of strength seemed to calm her entourage somewhat, and the chatter sparked back up around different corners of their tables as though nothing had actually happened.

'Come on, drink up. We have to leave in 10 minutes. They've cleared the road, so the journey will be 12 minutes,' said a gesturing Kelly, his right shirt sleeve pulled up to show the map broadcast down his arm, and the location of their ride underneath the skyscraper.

'You OK with the set list, Suki?' boomed Bob. 'Here, have another look,' he said as he elongated his arm to point his finger at the window pane, the once opaque night sky now filling with his projection of the set list, a dozen songs she knew off by heart in any case, as she feigned interest at the window, all the while stirring her olive around for the millionth time.

'Are we opening with 'Dreamer' again, Bob?' she grumpily chirped, the big gulp of water having shifted her malaise and indifference somewhat.

'Of course, dear. It really gets the crowd going and besides, it's too late to change now. We've already set the program for the lights at the start.'

Her wrist buzzed as her own arm now lit up with a reminder. Water. Ah, yes, performing was going to be stressful, and hot. And the two cocktails had sapped her desired pH levels, meaning she needed to drink 300 ml of water in the next five minutes.

The elevator did not make a sound, the view still incredible as the metal wall opened up to reveal Singapore's night sky once again as she descended to the car. The Tesla Model 33230 was indeed a stylish beast, a new age Ferrari of automation, comfort, and a metronomic accuracy record. From the GoogleHealth integration, she knew her water balance was now good and the HIM's research enabled her favourite media to sync from home to the car. Her choice this evening: a recording of her last concert, by the park in Sydney, during which 150,000 people had braved the outside world at night, no less, to marvel at her stage genius. Tesla cars were never late, never too hot or cold, and never failed to sync with your world. They just... worked! They were the cars of the rich and famous. Since they had bought out Ferrari in the late twenties, they had cornered the executive market, and were now way too expensive to ever be a GCab or be hired or owned by anyone less than a multi-millionaire.

Winding around the streets of Bugis, crossing Nicoll Highway and on towards the stadium, the in-car review of her last gig was interrupted by a security alert:

'WARNING!'

Her entourage of cars at once surrounded her own. She was seeing scenes of panic and of people being crushed up the stairs as though ants were swarming out of their nest, faces filled with panic and terror. *CNN* burst to life on the dash and reported some sort of public transport 'event', a failure of some description, right there in Singapore. Reports of explosions and of trains simply being 'stuck', terrified passengers bailing through the smoke-filled tunnels and trying to find their way above ground. Since the privatisation of most of the world's public transport, who else but Google had a 100 per cent record for safety and punctuality over 10 years!

'What on earth is going on?' shrieked Kelly, who seemed infinitely more panicked than Suki, who seemed, well, in a trance.

'Six minutes to the destination.'

'Tesla, defence formation with the pack. Maximum speed,' he commanded as the cars hurtled forward in a magnificent swell, hitting well over 100 mph, despite being inches from each other. The protection formation was all computer-controlled and just, well, magnificent, having them swooping around corners at the optimum angle to avoid any in-car discomfort, the auto balanced suspension counter acting on the exterior movement.

'...each and every station is offline and no trains are moving. We can now go live to City Hall MRT....' Then the picture cut to thousands of people all running up the moving staircases, smoke, soot, terror in the eyes.

'Re-route, CIM. Avoid MRT stations. Get off Nicholl Highway. Maximum defence formation with the pack.'

The Tesla roared as they took a sharp left, the pack cars all following within inches in front and behind even though the speed through an urban zone was well in excess of 60—even around the ninety-degree corners so common in this city. Suki looked to her right and saw a street vendor struggle to pull his cart from the edge of the street up the step. The speed of the Tesla inches from him made the poor guy fall backwards and drop the cart, leaving cooked chickens and soup spilling onto the road. Geylang Road was filled with traditional Singaporean hawker stalls, family businesses going back generations, with a renowned reputation for amazing food, one of the stalls even getting a Michelin star back in the day.

'Come on, let's get inside,' screamed Kelly as they made for the 10-yard dash to the VIP suites. Too late, no time, as in an instant the BANG was heard.

Then the water came...

So much water, so hard, as though an angry God had just poured a bucket the size of London right over their heads. The weight of it sent Suki crashing to the ground before she was picked up in one swoop by the guards. And then they were inside, safe, though confused, and scared. And wet.

5 The Big Crash

The rain continued to bash against the cold glass of the Upper East Side. Joe was aware that he'd dozed, and had awoken with that metallic dry taste only a sudden sleep can give. Clicking his fingers towards the storm, back came *CNN*, screens rotating wildly, sometimes ticker, sometimes split into four, sometimes full screen as the sheer pace of the reports coming in globally were broadcast. More unexplained rain. More public services failing, trains stopping, traffic lights causing gridlock in the city, various Z-list celebs popping up on screen to give their account of what was going on.

He winced as he moved from his partially buried mark—half sofa and half cushion—as his still cut and bruised eye reminded him of the crash.

Incoming. Government call. Urgent?

A dozen suits appear on the screen, sharper than steel, all probing questions and embedded safety language. Legal wheels who made sure he was given a plausible explanation for the crash. Physical malfunction and simultaneous backup failure.

Right.

He clicked the call off a nanosecond after their questions had been answered, his slumber replaced with a renewed energy despite the long-forgotten pain that still lingered. Would have been classed as a mere scratch back in the day. Now the Government suits were all over his condition, and of course hacking into Joe's HIM and reading back the sensory detail to prove their points.

He was curious now, suspicious and uneasy, as were a bulk of the world's population, as the 'Summer of Strife' continued globally.

'Normal service has been resumed today in Singapore's MRT system where it is reported that a build-up of atmospheric pressure preceding the great storm may have blown some electrical exchanges, causing simultaneous backup failure...' The pictures showed a nervous-looking but calm group of business men descending the steps of Somerset station. The picture then flicked to Fifth Avenue, the giant screen showing pictures just in from the corner near to Central Park that drew you into the underground Apple World where a dozen or so cops were busy trying to sort out a traffic problem at a traffic light failure.

Something wasn't right.

'HIM, get me some food. I'll Uber Eat. What are today's preferred options?'

'Well, Joe, based on your optimum weight of 172.4 pounds, you are currently 2.3 pounds over, so a low-carb, zero-sugar option is recommended.'

The screen in front of him lit up with the Uber Eat logo, and a million different images all flashed by on the screen, finally settling on two choices from Joe's known favourites that the HIM had curated for him. He could have any one delivered in 20 minutes.

'I'll take the chicken and make sure it's hot. Extra pepper,' he said before moving to the fridge and chugging down a cold Pepsi while the screen confirmed the inventory deduction and the time to reorder, which he ignored. The 'bing' chime on the screen of the fridge gave him the good news of the 'Healthy Meal Choice +30 points' that would be added to his Life Points balance.

He'd been on paid leave for a week since the crash. Cabin fever had set in as he was assigned a series of meals and exercises each day to help him recover from the shock. They had even prescribed him a course of daily puzzles to ensure the good health of his cognitive function and recall.

Only, he *could* remember alright. Putting what he remembered with what was still playing on his media walls—*CNN* still garishly red against the grey and gloom of the real-life pictures they were showing. And it was not sitting easy with him.

Incoming.

'Joe, it's Sergeant Stokes. Should I connect?'

With a raised thumb, Joe didn't have to say anything, his central screen replacing *CNN* with that of Stokes, his long-standing buddy, who also happened to be his boss.

'Hey, buddy. How's the recovery coming along?'

Everyone was pussyfooting around him, and Joe couldn't hide his slight irritation with a quizzical frown and a dismissive tone.

'Listen, Joe, NYC is spooking everyone out, Singapore has people in bits, and these storms…'

Trying not to roll his eyes, Joe was still dismissive.

'…so we've a couple of options for you coming back soon. We're talking about a three-day week…' cue huge eyebrow frown—this time he couldn't help it, 'or how'd you fancy a moonlight with the Level 2 boys? Central Park and Times Square for a bit?'

The mood changed and the frown lit up into an eager twist, as though he'd just been given a million-dollar bonus. He couldn't hide this one either.

'But, but, my knee. They won't let me do anything other than Level 3.'

'Joe, it's all hands on deck right now, and besides, I… put in a word. See you tomorrow. Sending you some stuff now, Joe. Stand by.' And Stokes signed off with a grin as he knew he'd just made his buddy's day, if not his week or his year.

The early morning command car was functional and efficient. Kind of like a GCab but without the comfort. None of the things like media integration, but it was to get him from A to B, and fast. His morning shift started at 09.00, and he was to meet Stokes outside Apple World. Stokes, who was on secondment with the Fifth Avenue Level 2 Brigade, cut an imposing figure as the wave of uniforms parted—like Moses commanding the Red Sea—to allow the car through to the sidewalk.

'Jones. Over here,' boomed the sergeant, no time for pleasantries or emotion, which kind of spooked Joe a little, seeing as their 20-year history meant they were more best buddies than anything else.

'Sir.'

'Good to see you, Jones. Situation is calm now, but it may not stay that way for long, so fall in with the guys over here, B Squad, and I'll have someone explain the crowd control tactics we will deploy.'

'Sir.'

The guys, standing to his right where Stokes had indicated B Squad was, all looked the part. While Joe had the same gear which had been couriered to him via drone earlier that day, he didn't feel like he owned the uniform. As if to put him at ease, one of the crew came over and patted him on the helmet, cam bouncing downwards slowly under the weight of the gentle pat, and Joe's rig indicated that this was Jose Hurtado, section lead.'

'Nice to meet you, Jose. Where do you need me?'

'You'll be my wingman, Jones. Stick to my right. Everything is calm right now, but it could all go off in a second, man. We are hoping for some reinforcements soon. I guess you are the start of those.'

The road was deserted of traffic, save for *lots* of uniform. And an eerie buzz surrounded the early morning skies, a buzz made up of people, birds, weather and well, something intangible. You could just feel the tension all around. All it would take would be a trigger event, and this could just go off.

With a stomach so tight, Joe struggled to recall this type of feeling. Like the nerves you have as your horse comes on to the shoulder of the leader with a furlong to go. Like when your team gets a field goal from 52 yards with 0.2 left on the clock. Like the time that Benji had to go to hospital to have his leg operated on when he totalled his bike. The feeling was part nauseous hangover, part dehydrated thirst, part lovesick teenage angst waiting for the SMS to come back.

The screens here were everywhere in the sky, advertising a plethora of targeted goods and services depending on just who was nearby, and who had eyes on at that particular moment. And of course, *CNN* had to have a screen somewhere, as if it had become the ubiquitous voice of the nation, far and away the #number one news resource globally now. President Trump in his second term had relaxed the monopolisation bills in the mid-twenties, which had allowed *CNN* to merge with *Fox* and provide a coverage no one else on the planet could rival. The merger itself was very controversial, like bringing two warring nations together as one after years being on the other side of the fence. Nonetheless, it had happened, money proving once again that it can trump ideology and politics at any point if the price is right.

The 'Summer of Strife' was still the #number one story, and a myriad tickers and screens moved from Sydney to London to Singapore in an instant, all reporting on the strange 'simultaneous backup failures' that seemed to be failing public transport, along with the worsening weather 'events'. This time another monsoon causing unbelievable flooding in Hong Kong.

Joe stood stock-still, surveying the scene, trying not to get sucked into the screens above when he should have been watching the people, the masses, looking for micro signs of movement, of someone behaving oddly, of unrest heading towards their locale at the South East corner of Central Park just up from Trump Tower. The previous day the store he was now guarding, Apple World, had been looted just after noon as a gang of seemingly uncoordinated individuals had torn into the store and just started ripping devices from tables. Just 15 minutes and the store was a wreck, police powerless to help, even though a few shots got fired. Thankfully no one was hurt. It was the first 'riot' in NYC for 15 years.

'BREAKING NEWS.'

'Wall Street has suspended trading for the first time in 18 years this morning at 11.00 due to a reported DDOS attack, this just after the circuit breaker was activated due to a flash crash caused by automated and systemic high frequency trading…'

Trigger.

Instinct took over as the first rush happened. A huge right hand was deflected by the bulk of the shield. The assailant slumped to the ground as the low frequency sound wave gun kicked in, emitted directly from the shield as it was struck, rendering the attacker immobile as the sound waves attacked the respiratory system. The guy was now sitting on the sidewalk struggling for air. Not that Joe had time to process it as another one came. Same result. Then another. And Joe took a blow to his temple that momentarily knocked a gap in the wall of police before the guys in his company retreated as instructed by their rigs into the testudo formation, all shields and tortoise-style defence, which, after a few minutes seemed to work, rendering an end to a buzz that Joe hadn't felt for years. An actual fight, actual disorder: so much more engaging than the point and serve tactics he had deployed as a Level 3 out in the burbs.

The police spread out from the tortoise shell shape now, back into a line facing the protesters. Joe surveyed the scene again as a hush descended on the street itself against the ferocious backdrops of the screens above, which were still peddling their wares. The crowd was angry, but also seemed to be kind of dirty: a real mix of young and old, grime on their faces and their clothes. Where had these people come from?

Joe caught a glimpse of an older guy, easily in his 50s, as he held a wooden makeshift sign that was a simple cross and a square piece on the front with the slogan 'Global governments have killed us for years' daubed in purple paint, as if that was all he'd had in his garage when he knocked it up. Beside him was an even angrier boy in his early 20s wearing huge boots, but, though dishevelled, he was fully made-up as if he was going to appear on TV, his grimace extenuating the effect of his black eyeliner and giving him a really haunting look.

Their anger shook Joe a little as he hadn't really seen poverty for a while, not with his job and the cautious overseeing of Monica, meaning his time at work or even away from work was safe in the grass verges of the burbs.

All in all, it took 15 minutes for the situation to restore itself, and a series of officers regularly engaged in controlling tactics to ensure the crowd remained still. And then they dispersed ever so slightly.

The screens moved now from advertising to information, as if someone had flicked a switch and changed them all to a different channel. The odd numbered screens continued to show the chaos on Wall Street—which was now calming—as the even numbered screens displayed a huge 'TRADING SUSPENDED' ticker that continued to scroll across them all, knocking the live coverage out— which then came back on a few seconds later like a rolling wall of information. Yes, it was news, but there was almost an instructional feel to the screens behaving like this. It was as if someone was implying 'Go home' with the news that Wall Street was down. Wall Street hardly ever crashed. It had never, ever gone fully down, not since the Great Fire of 1835, which was 203 years ago, unless you could count the J.P. Morgan explosion in 1929 that caused trading to be stopped for a short time. The crash of 2008 had also halted trading for a short time. The last episode had been in the early twenties when the Covid outbreak had caused chaos. This had also halted trading.

Break time. Five minutes. Water was needed according to his arm, but Joe had other things in mind.

'Call Monica.'

She came into view in the upper corner of his police-issue GGlasses. She was at home, kitchen in the background just visible, as was Benji over her shoulder. He was sitting at the table, engaging in some old school board games, which were nowadays the holographic type. Visible was some kind of small table-sized mountain, on which stood at various heights and points across it some animal figures, all fighting to see who could get to the top fastest.

'Where are you?' Monica spoke, and was looking worried.

'Listen, I don't have much time, I'm downtown, Manhattan.'

Joe had never called like this before the split, when she'd grown bored and started attending after-hours groups with the crowd from work looking, well… for someone to share her interests. She'd had enough of Joe's risk-taking and his laissez-faire attitude to the parenting of Benji, since he'd lost his…will.

Loving her child so much meant the possibility of a long life for them together, and that was something that appealed to her, especially since she'd lost her parents so young, so fitness became the thing and it consumed her. And Josh too. And when she fell away from Joe, she had grown closer to Josh, and the train was set in motion. The boulder was rolling down the hill, and the split happened. She felt guilty, and deep down she still loved Joe, enough to keep

Josh at arm's length and not make the split absolute, in so much as the new totally replaced the old. There was no living together, just dating, and just casual. Not that any of that mattered to Joe, who had reacted badly. Petulant and brooding, he had retreated to his own work and his new place with the mod cons overlooking the city. Monica's nest egg from her parents' accident had paid for that, and her guilt had made her agree that they would share the rent for a year before they figured out what to do.

'Listen, you have to get out, you have to go. Take Benji. You can be at my mom and dad's in a few hours, I'll have the GCab come collect you both. I'll stump up the cash, so don't worry. Just take enough clothes for a couple of weeks and then things will have settled down.'

'What are you *talking* about, Joe?' said Monica.

'Seriously, Monica, please don't argue. I know we haven't seen eye to eye, but you don't know what's going on. I don't like this: my accident, the riots, Wall Street, the weird weather. I've been drafted to Level 2 and I'm here in the riot and I don't like it, Monica. I don't like it a bit.'

6 London Zombies

The events on the rotating screens in his bedroom were incredible.

'Get back!' roared a police officer, and the camera panned across his fear and towards the crowds.

The scene was like one of those old movies they showed on the History channel and in schools. A snarling mass of bodies and hands flailing like claws, eyes on stalks as though a zombie plague had just taken over, except their clothes were slightly more modern and neater. New York Police and US Army together with sonic riot shields knocking them down like skittles, but the sheer weight of numbers were pushing the lines back and back. Huge trucks, all armour and impossibly large tyres, were actually electrical cannons firing pulse waves, which flung the zombies high into the air and back down again. Being winded was the best-case scenario, if no bones took a pounding on the way down. The screen panned into the crowd at a hilarious 'undead creature' that looked out of place, too young to be there, 16 or 17 years old. He stood tall with a two-tone hairpiece that was flat to the left and back, combed high to the right, asymmetric to the extreme, and this was set off by the same look all the way down. He had one large earring and one small one; bright red on one half of the mouth and pastel colour on the other; half a jacket and half a blouse; denim jean on one leg and trouser on the other; one shoe and one boot. Oh, how the young ached to be individual these days. This one was the perfect embodiment of two people, as if schizophrenia had suddenly become common *and* cool. The half-face told lies in its rage as both halves contorted the same way. Both jean and trouser leg crunched the pavement in a charge that was part rabid, part manic zombie, firing forward to meet the crunch of the sonic shield. This was followed by the ear-splitting, if inaudible, sound wave as both halves hit the road with a gasp for one breath to fill out two lungs.

All this as the traffic lights failed. It showed just how dependant we had become on technology. It also showed an intrinsic fear of the authorities. Years and years of peace, of things just... working, and all of a sudden, the masses see the streets controlled by police again. In riot gear? It was like fear breeding fear. The uncertainty of the police, the lack of training and real-life experience they all had of real disorder, of crowd control, was transmitted to the public, who in turn projected their own fears back. And violence was the only certainty today.

Dylan's room was bare, yet strangely lived in. His routine comprised shifting from his bed to his desk to his screens to his wardrobes and to his computer station. It was full of electronics, sparse of clothes and character. Yet this was a room that he spent all his time in. The personalised memo screen above workstation one gave way to his full name: Dylan Ryan Montgomery. At least six screens were spread across his desk, a seriously impressive manual rig that at least hinted at the talent which sat in front of it.

Dylan had a solitary poster. Just the one. On old school shiny paper, held in place by even older school tacks, her face constantly looked down and connected to him. Her androgynous features and bright blonde hair gave way to a sexuality beyond his years, or maybe not, as she was his fantasy and his dreams.

Suki.

He got up from his bed where the TV flickered off to reveal his day's to-do list before a flick of the wrist in the direction of the screen had *CNN* back on. It was showing the zombies live from London that afternoon, on The Mall itself as the demonstrators somehow wanted to fight the police right in front of the King, as if to show William that they meant business.

The crowds there seemed a little cleaner, if no less mad. It was as if the grime of New York trumped the grime of London. Or perhaps the late September rain in London had washed the faces of the zombies. Dylan had been a big fan of zombie movies, the old classics such as *Dawn of the Dead* paling into comparison against modern masterpieces like *28 Days Later*, and he recognised the slow, jerky movements of some of the characters advancing down the wide avenue towards the palace. The police had set a perimeter some way from the usual places that pedestrians could go, for fear of any sorts of missiles, bombs or explosives going the way of the building itself. That the flag was not flying did not matter, this was the symbolic residence of the monarchy the world over, and heaven forbid that any nutter would try to sabotage or damage it.

Drones whizzed overhead capturing ever more footage of the crowds, no doubt to follow up in the coming days with arrest warrants for those who could be identified. The West had steadfastly refused to bring in facial recognition by way of population control like the Chinese had in the early to mid-twenties. It was instead being used to 'investigate crimes', which was just the Government's way of trying to say, 'No, we are not using it' when in reality they meant, 'Well, we are not using it officially, but we will use it when we want to. And if you are doing anything wrong, then we will use it to find you, and it was your fault anyway so no, we won't apologise for using it then.'

Dylan saw even more half-faces in the London crowd. Surely this was a global trend now, and he shook his head at the madness of it all. He was pleased that people were rising up, and one day they'd remember his name as being the catalyst for it all. But he couldn't stand some of the characters in the world nowadays, their duplicitousness, their deceit, the way they openly espoused hypocritical shite like loving the planet but loving their lithium battery-operated cars more. It had long been proven that mining cobalt from the depths of the earth beneath the Congo was way more catastrophic than the micro pollutants of the very early twentieth-century combustion engines, but the Liberal cabal that ruled the world eventually twisted even that narrative towards the economic growth of Africa being a good thing.

Settling into his workstation, the myriad screens flickered with an array of code, save for one, which had another live feed, like that earlier of Fifth Avenue, New York. He grinned as the skirmishes broke out before switching his focus back to the trade boards, the markets open and ready for the bounce, which would make him very, very rich. The algorithms had been perfect, driving the prices of certain stocks all over the place, making it very easy for him to play both bear and bull and wait for the inevitable settling effect, which would occur once the markets came back up. His tracks were covered expertly, the information in The Book worth every single penny of what he had paid for it: lists of code, algorithms, backdoor entries into the world of Google and the US Department of Transport. Where it had come from who knew? He didn't care, but in his skilled hands, he was able to wreak havoc, confident that his firewalls and daisy-chain IP routes would confuse even the most sophisticated of trackers.

He was convinced that Wall Street was going to go down soon, so he worked fast to manoeuvre his trades and then move around the funds. The markets were indeed in a tail spin, and the riots occurring certainly did not help matters. It was a little after 15.00 his time, and Wall Street had only been open 30 minutes. Already stocks were crashing left right and centre as investors tried to get their cash and liquidise themselves as much as possible.

His remote trades were highly elaborate, all conceived via a tangled web of companies worldwide. The time spent studying not only the markets, but also the oversight on global financial institutions, meant that Dylan knew exactly how to get money in and out quickly, and how to maximise his returns. He'd built up a sizeable nest egg that he'd managed to hide from the authorities thus far, and had also resisted the temptation to spend it, figuring that his plan was the only thing that mattered. And it was now time to move into full deployment of that plan.

It started with the GoogleCab. Just a quick write of malicious code was enough to make that one car stop talking to that set of traffic lights. And BAM... accident! Then it was time to see what else he could do. Previously researched backdoor entries into the Google-backed public services saw him test the waters further with the train incident in Singapore. Then the traffic lights in NYC.

That was a hilarious test. The previous night had played out just as he had hoped it would. First, a few sets in downtown Manhattan caused hilarious scenes as GCabs bucked and wailed like wild horses trying to figure out which way to turn and when to move and when to stop. There had been a few casualties for sure, but his clear lack of empathy and guilt, pointing to a narcissistic and psychopathic set of tendencies, simply thought of it as collateral damage.

The scene from the city cams he hacked was hilarious, and he had roared with laughter just as if he had been watching a classic slapstick movie in which its characters were falling over themselves. The cars were acting like crazy and playing games of chicken and dodgeball with the pedestrians running hither and thither.

This of course only fuelled the unrest of the crowd, not that he could know about that, or even sense it, but because the oft quoted folly, *The Madness of Crowds,* was right: that fool would follow fool. After all, it was back as far the mid-1630s that the world had seen tulip bulbs become one of the most expensive items on the planet. Fools indeed.

The madness of this particular crowd was fuelled by uncertainty, by propaganda, by the combination of the Government controlling the narrative on one hand and the conspiracy theorists the other hand. It was slowly driving the lambs—who trusted their farmers as the hand that fed them—mad. People just didn't know who or what to believe.

All of this led Dylan up to the BIG ONE: Wall Street.

This was just Phase One of his plan though. He had way bigger things to achieve than Wall Street, and besides, what use was money in this horrific world if you had no one with you to spend it, to enjoy it? And humanity was killing itself anyway, so he wanted out. Away from it all.

He had his back story figured out: an alter ego of passport, bank accounts and a social media stack that gave his new alter ego, Dylan David Norris, just the right amount of gravitas in case of a story search by the Feds. He had worried that keeping his Christian name could put him in jeopardy if someone, somewhere made two and two equal four, but he figured that risk paled into insignificance against the difficulty of learning, and possibly forgetting, a new Christian name, during airport searches or security stops.

David was his father's name, though he didn't really know him very well. He knew that he had left them all alone when he was ten, and that his mother didn't really like to talk about him anymore. But he'd seen the odd photo here and there, and he often wondered what had been so bad in their world that his father had just upped and left. His mother had said he was a terrible man, and though the details were sketchy, Dylan did kind of remember arguments between them; his father working a lot and then going out a lot; and things like holidays or family treats being very rare. There was that time at the seaside he remembered, but it all went sour when he got spooked by a seagull trying to steal his chips and he'd fallen sideways into his dad and spilled his carton all over the pavement too. That ended up with a shouting match between his mum and dad and it was all somehow Dylan's fault for being clumsy.

Flicking between the closing prices of the stocks on screen one and the rapidly moving prices now that the markets had just reopened on screen two, to the sell instructions on screen three, to his bank accounts on screen four, the dollars continued to roll in for Dylan. Not huge sums in one place, nothing to leave a trail, but $500k here and a million there. The $250k on a manufacturer of police riot shields tickled him as the profit flashed by on the screen. Worldwide demand was soaring now! His biggest chuckle came on seeing the $1.2 million from the portable traffic light supplier that had suddenly become inundated with orders since the original failures the previous week in NYC.

Flicking another screen to his travel plans, he got up and moved to his case to check his belongings for his trip to see his world. His precious next day's flight to NYC to meet her was oh so close, and his plans had worked, his bank accounts filled and moved and moved through various chains all disguised with IP re-routing protocols so no one could ever work it back to him.

New York. Tomorrow.

Time to hide his case in case his mother came in. And time for sleep.

7 You Must Leave This Area

Adams woke with a start. Gesturing to the wall, on flicked the news with a rolling story about the seemingly global phenomenon of storms being some kind of freak weather pattern that happens once every hundred years, something to do with solar alignment.

General James Adams III was a big deal in the US Military. A career military veteran, he'd been born and raised in Sherburne County, Minnesota, and received a bachelor's degree in aerospace engineering from the United States Military Academy. He saw active service in Iraq in the 2000s, and had been appointed the previous year to head up Central Command, which included a lot of special projects such as RO707, which was of huge strategic importance to the entire US Military. Nail this, establish a revenue stream for other NATO or affiliated territories, and he was sure he'd get his next and final bump up the chain and possibly eventually even that fifth star he so craved.

Adams being of a certain generation, still had a personal device, which he swore by for confidentiality reasons. Even the military couldn't persuade him to part with it and were constantly trying to keep it patched and updated. He picked it up from the bedside table, and smiled at his home screen as he saw his precious family in front of the fire and the tree the previous Christmas. Family time was the reason he got up in the morning. His childhood sweetheart looked much younger than her 52 years on this planet. She was resplendent in the blue and red Christmas family jumper. Natalie, his wife now of 27 years, had given him four amazing kids. James IV was the eldest at 22, with twins Melanie and Michelle looking absolutely radiant at 19, and the youngest was Jude, who was 17 and almost as tall as his father.

'Good morning, General—'

'Call me Jim, please,' he interrupted before the hotel AutoButler could go on, 'and I'll have my usual coffee: large pint, 84°, 10 per cent half and half, two sugars please, china mug, stirred four times.'

A few seconds later, the wall unit beeped and out rolled a freshly ordered cup of coffee, exactly as he had requested.

CNN was rolling back to the scenes of the previous night in NYC where the stock markets had reopened and the streets at least were a little calmer. A presidential address from Obama flashed by on another screen where her always immaculate stoic friendliness appealed for calm, as only a 74-year-old grandmother could. Yet there seemed a hint of tiredness behind her eyes, perhaps sadness at the passing of Barack the year before, or perhaps the almost 40 years in politics taking their toll on her gait.

Shower done, sports casual wear on and clicking his fingers whilst at the same time saying the name 'Robinson' caused the screen in front of him to appear and he summoned his assistant, Marsha, who answered the call with, 'Sir!' as though she had a point to prove to the boss.

'We're going live, Robinson. Get ready to depart after breakfast. I'm going for a V-Run along Mulholland, then we can leave the hotel at 07.50. Make the arrangements for the flight would you. Leave by 09.00 local time. We need to be on Fifth by 08.00 New York time, and I want the first test run by nine. Is that clear, Robinson?' Not pausing for an answer, he added, 'Make it happen.' Wrist flick. Robinson disappeared and the news replaced her.

Mulholland time now. Adams donned the suit, flicked on the helmet and entered the grab circle, the floor moving and lifting as he started to run, all the while snapping and clicking and barking orders for his rig to simulate his favourite LA street. '...and make it morning time, 06.30, temperature 18°C, wind 10 mph from the south please,' he said as the AC jets kicked a swirl of cool towards him and he pushed off step by step up the hill from the Hollywood Bowl and began to run.

The car to the airport had been easy with Robinson handling logistics on her rig while Adams took the main console and woke a seemingly endless succession of people in New York with the news of, 'We're going live. Get ready.' The car pulled right in to Domodedovo Airport, efficiently taking care of the security protocols with a series of scanner-to-scanner mini battles at the checkpoints, worm-like creatures protruding from both bonnet and security gate beeping and lasering each other like spitting cobras being fluted out of the basket.

Passing the side gate, Adams and Robinson exited the car right beside the aircraft, the rest of the team following as they boarded. Inside, the walls all appeared transparent, which made it look as if the seats they took were floating in mid-air. A few orderlies fussed around and then the walls changed, the temperature dropped, and each person was now in their own fully functioning SleepPod, ready to catch some chem sleep to adjust the body clock for the seven-hour time change. Leave Moscow 09.00, arrive almost two hours earlier, ready once again for breakfast, no jet lag.

Robinson shifted nervously in her seat. The copter they'd transferred to on landing was smooth enough. The view over Manhattan was surreal, the visible surge of the masses right on Fifth, pushing north towards the corner of Central Park right into the pulsating chink of light of the riot shields and smoke and fires. Utter chaos. Further south towards Wall Street, there was another wave of protestors, no doubt blaming the bankers and 'the institution' for everything that was happening right now.

Scenes like this had not been seen in New York since, well, since she couldn't even remember. Though the sheer volume of people reminded her of those Pride Marches that used to take place back in the day when being LGBT was not quite as commonplace as it was now.

'We're going to land in the park. ETA three minutes. Stand by,' she crackled in her headphones, and the soldiers shifted their guns nervously from one shoulder to the other as Adams made adjustments to his helmet.

Down.

'Go, go, go, go.'

Forward now, the downwash from the rotors made standing balance difficult, however the chain of the troops helped Adams and Robinson move in unison towards the huge truck parked opposite The Pierre, which was to be their sanctuary.

The monitors literally hummed below the crisp day glow lights. Soldiers on chairs were surveying the wreckage a little further down the avenue, piloting the drones that delivered the up-to-date intel. Robinson touched the side of her head as the GGlasses sprang to life, making the names of each solider apparent as she walked towards Stokes.

'Sergeant Stokes, I'm Marsha Robinson, please stand to attention for General Adams.'

'Sir!' Cue locking of feet and a crisp salute. 'We are holding the crowd at the intersection of 59th, sir, but we need to move on dispersion tactics and get these people out of the area.'

'OK, Stokes, listen up, there's a reason I'm here, and it's because of my special project. Robinson and I will oversee matters from now on. You can brief the teams. There's a new squadron coming to town and you need to know what it is, who they are and how you work with them.'

'Yes sir. Understood sir. Awaiting further instructions.'

Realising that something big was being explained, Joe gently tugged the arm of his wingman, Hurtado, and moved a couple of paces very discreetly towards Stokes, his CO noticing the movement out the corner of his eye but ignoring it. After all they went way back, and with your backs to a wall, you wanted those you could trust around you.

'We are ready to deploy a squadron of autonomous bots to your command, Sergeant Stokes. Code name RO707. They are the latest and greatest thing in police and military issue crowd control and they have been extensively tested on simulated ops around the world.'

'Simulated, sir?' Stokes couldn't help himself and cut in. Adams had been braced for it, experience telling him that if Stokes was in command here, he was good, and a good cop or a good soldier should ask that question.

'Yes, sergeant. Today is the first real-life deployment, which is why I've flown straight in from Moscow with my chief of staff, Robinson. She will be your first point of contact, and the bots are establishing her presence in your HUD now via your rig. Is that clear?'

'Understood, sir, and welcome ma'am. I have you now in my HUD.'

Although less than 40 feet from him, over his shoulder Robinson was now an avatar in his field of vision, temporarily made bigger when she was speaking and moving surreptitiously back when not required.

'OK, Stokes, here is the sit rep. We've programmed the bots to imitate your men in so much as they have been fed your entire operating manual. They know your protocol, your orders and will be acting as police in this exercise, not as full military officers. We will deploy a squadron in the centre of the moving crowd, down towards 52nd from 58th. They will have orders to gain control of the cross sections across Fifth and will be advising the crowd to leave the area. Is that understood?'

'Yes ma'am,' complied Stokes as his chest tightened and the reality of some form of battle kicked in.

Robinson continued: 'Assign a couple of units with them to monitor their performance please. I'll stay on the HUD and coordinate with the bot leading the squad. Hurtado, Jones, Bot Squad 1,' and scanning further, 'Ramirez, Aspall, you guys are Squad 2. All four of you connect directly to my rig, please, and I'll approve.'

Joe felt his own heart leap at the excitement of what was to come. It was a far cry from his day to day of recent times, and robots no less. Androids maybe. Whatever. This was scary, but cool. Trying to portray an outer calm, he fell in towards Hurtado's right arm this time and slipped him the tiniest of winks to signify that he was up for this.

Adams interrupted. 'Robinson, have you got the screens in hand yet? When can we communicate with the crowd, and tell them of… the consequences?'

'Yes, sir. We are a couple of minutes away max. The RO707s will be the main message with anyone caught on the side street facing a mandatory month in the clink. That's if our guys don't immobilise them first.'

The CyberTrucks pulled up all of a sudden from around the corner towards Central Park. Five, six, seven, all screeching to a halt and hitching low on their front wheels, the roof peeling upwards from the back like some sort of mad beetle undergoing a metamorphosis and revealing its wings as it bowed low to the floor. What emerged from the back of the truck that headed for the sky was something incredible. Like chrome gods the bots emerged in groups of four and moved elegantly in lockstep with each other and then quickly off down Fifth in an easy formation, rifles pulled and pointed strongly towards anyone that shouldn't be there—which was everyone that wasn't real police or a military officer.

Following at a safe distance behind, Stokes gestured to the next corner to draw attention to the incoming surge of protestors. Hurtado clocked it and saw in his own rig that the magnificent robots were smashing through the first gathering on the corner of 57th, each bot immobilising four people at once with a simple electric stun to the back of the neck. And then they were carried away, one person to one arm and gently set in the makeshift quarantine zone that another squad of human police had set up before the bots returned to the melee for another four. Impressive and scary when coupled with the associated booming sound of:

'YOU MUST LEAVE THIS AREA NOW! FAILURE TO DO SO WILL RESULT IN A JAIL SENTENCE.

YOU MUST LEAVE THIS AREA NOW! FAILURE TO DO SO WILL RESULT IN A JAIL SENTENCE.

CAPTURE BY A POLICE BOT WILL RESULT IN A SAFE STUN. YOU HAVE BEEN WARNED. LEAVE NOW.'

'Joe, we are going live on the screens in T minus 60 seconds. Bot warning. Please confirm your teams are ready from 58th to 52nd. Over.'

Stokes was still on the corner of 58th, but his rig was portraying all the action he needed to see at each intersection, and he could see that Jones and Hurtado were quickening their pace now, being a little behind schedule, and were scrambling to get to 52nd as quickly as they could.

Joe hit the corner first a few seconds in front of Hurtado, both of them behind another group of four bots who had the codes G7, G9, G11 and G12 in place of a name. He spun around on the spot and faced back up the street towards 58th, an unconscious reaction to a past human time when it was usual to look at your subject when talking.

'Sir, yes sir. We are ready. Estimate 1,000 protestors per side street, and I'll need four more bots on the south side of the avenue here ready to hold and immobilise if required. Side streets secured by the bots. No one getting through them into the avenue now, sir.'

Suddenly the camera view moved dramatically. Tarmac filled the screen as the noise boomed through the speakers and the smoke shifted in view.

Explosion.

'Jones, sit rep, come in!' boomed Stokes as Adams and Robinson moved out of the way of the panicked sergeant. Footage on the HUD from one of the drones took their attention as Joe struggled to get back up. The window of the now destroyed clothing store was shooting glass out into the street while smoke filled the area. Some of the crowd were ducking for cover and some who were pre-prepped with bandanas over mouths and hands in the air, clearly got the memo while others didn't. There'd clearly been a group hiding inside one of the stores ready to attack and outflank. They had planted the bomb to cause maximum disruption and were now attempting to wade through the cordon of stunned police. Only they hadn't reckoned on coming up against 20 odd tonnes of moveable, breathable, yet super strong metallic compound-clad robots, who instantly retreated half a block and collected Ramirez and Aspall, who had been that side of the street. They didn't look too hurt, only dazed, and Joe was quick to get back onto comms on the HUD.

'Explosion, sir. Robinson, ma'am, you need to deploy the bots in a hold mode. We have to drive the crowd back as one. When they disappear to put people in the containment areas, it's leaving gaps in the formation. Let's get this area cleared and secured.'

8 Heading for the Concert

'Suki, ma'am, I have the results of your morning's bio-sample analysis, and I'm prepping today's medication.'

The eloquent tones of Barbara, the British female RoboButler, worked fast as Suki made her way from the bathroom back to the huge white Egyptian bed. Her silk robe matched the elegance of the surroundings and her wet hair flicked back over the bed as she reclined and sighed loudly.

The doors opened and Kelly came towards her with a smile, orange juice in hand.

'Morning, darling. How are you feeling?'

No response. No movement. Her resting bitch face at its worst.

'Big night tonight. Final concert. Hope they sort out all... that.' Kelly motioned to the window with his hand and up came *CNN* again, live from downtown, which was now deserted, save for the huge military presence.

'Mmm, yeah,' she sighed again, rolling over with outstretched hand to get the juice. A large gulp and it was half gone. A big smile came from Kelly following the liquid into her system.

'I put something in to, er, make you feel good,' he confessed. Her RBF turned back on in an instant.

'Really, is that all you men can think about, when things like *this* are happening? Get lost.'

A new powerful version of Viagra for women was the drug of choice sweeping the world. Designed to improve the female libido within minutes and promoted and sold by governments at a loss-leading price in an effort to propel the falling birth rates, Dialezide was *the* designer chemical of choice that year. While the top of the range MedButlers would still divvy out a thrice daily concoction of the good stuff: Zoloft, Ritalin, Prozac—uppers, downers, liveners, sleepies—whatever you needed, Dialezide was very much a manual drug controlled by men who wanted what they needed.

Beating a retreat, Suki ignored him as she switched off the screens and had daylight enter her hotel room. The views across the rest of Brooklyn towards the venue to her right and to her left, were a curious vision of a familiar skyline that just somehow felt different. The odd plume of smoke gave a tell-tale rise to the activities that had ravaged Manhattan in the last 24 hours.

'I'm going for a bath. Barbara, I need a Furo. Please prep it for me: 43°, just how I like it. Kelly, you can go and get lost. You can put as much Dialezide into my juice as you want. Doesn't mean I have to enjoy myself with *you*. I'll take care of myself thanks, so get lost.'

Tantrum, towels thrown, Kelly beat a smiling retreat as his imagination kicked in and he reversed through the door for fear of another projectile going straight for his head.

Kelly wasted no time in getting prepped for his new content. His hands whirled in front of him as he asked Barbara to set the lights in the living room of the penthouse to the optimum setting for one of his 'off the cuff' videos. Since the announcement of his engagement to Suki, his channels had gone into overdrive. There was as much trolling as there were new fans, but with the clicks and views came the riches. His agent was fielding yet more endorsement calls since the news had broken, no doubt with fans of Suki's target market rather than his own, and his reach was now being exploded due simply to the person he was betrothed to.

'Well, hello gang. Just thought I'd throw you some new content. Look. At. This…' he shrieked at an uncommonly high pitch as he twirled in front of the huge window overlooking the city. The blink just above the screen as well as the one on his rig indicated that he was recording on two screens at once.

'Today is the day. It's Suki's last ever concert.' Fist in mouth in faux surprise, as he continued to ham up his narrative as though he'd never had a day's acting lessons in his life. Well, he hadn't. And he sure was a ham.

'So we are prepping right now. Suki is getting ready, shhhhhh, she's in the bath. Oh no, you can't go in and see, you naughty people, hahahahaha,' he announced as he continued to mince and flounce. 'So, anyway, we hope to see you all at the Barclays Center tonight in Brooklyn. It's going to be *epic*, and I think there are still five, yes *five,* VIP premium video experiences up for grabs if you subscribe to my channel in the next hour and upgrade to premium. *And* you'll be in the draw! I really hope to see you there. It's gonna be great!'

Silence.

His face dropped as fast as his mood, his hands whirling again as he talked to Barbara and made some posting and editing decisions on the spot. Then, settling back into the huge sofa, he kicked his heels over onto the coffee table, and Barbara played the final edit.

'For your approval, sir,' she announced and awaited a response.

Kelly's mind wandered to the scene he could imagine in the bathroom right now. It took all his might for him to stay seated on the sofa as he knew Suki too well, and he needed to let her cool off rather than force his will onto her, however 'hot' she may have been feeling due to his little potion.

'Confirmed, Barbara. But please don't post yet. Please send to Tony and ask him for approval before posting. In fact, call Tony and I'll tell him you're sending it now.'

'As you wish, sir. Calling Tony now.'

In a second, his manager, confidant and long-time collaborator, Tony G, appeared on the screen, apparently still in bed, but thankfully alone.

'Hey Kelly. What's up?'

'You lazy fucker, come on dude, get your head in the game. Big day today. I'm just sending you a quick post to approve and then my HIM here is gonna post it. Can you do that?'

'Yeah, whatever. I'll get going soon. It's gonna be a long night, man. I need all the rest I can get, hahaha. Have you ordered any Hydration Stations for later?'

'Nah, man. Fuck that. I got my guy on the West Side standing by to feed me a fake test, so we can just skip it. Let's get properly fucked up, man. It is Suki's last concert after all.'

'Fuck off, Kelly. If you believe that, you will believe anything. Yeah, I get her clock is ticking and she wants a kid, or maybe even two. You want to hope that jizz you froze when you were a kid is still active, man. I bet it's got freezer burn by now. No way will you be able to give her what she wants. And besides, you *hate* kids. And when she gets them, she'll realise that she misses the music and she'll be right back at it.'

'Jesus, you *are* in a state this morning! Someone have bad dreams, did they? Just fucking approve my post and I'll see you later, but this time make sure you are cheered the heck up!'

Kelly flicked his middle finger at the screen as he tapped the rim of his rig with the other hand and started to laugh to himself.

Kelly was a native of New York, born Jeremy Pietersen in the Upper East Side of Manhattan, son to his father, a government official, and mother, Amy, who was a particularly bohemian artist. Raised in the 'free' twenty-teens when everything was coffee shops, and doing what you wanted whenever you wanted, Kelly had bought into a very spirited ethos from his mother, to whom he was very close. LGBTQ+ had just really come alive as a global movement then, and he was encouraged to talk about his feelings at a very young age, though he was a sullen little boy who clung to his mother. His absent workaholic father was always at some council meeting or other, so he got to attend his mother's art classes and long lunches with a very eclectic crowd. His transition to become Kelly at the age of six left little in the memory, save for the fact that he knew it had put a huge strain on his parent's marriage and they had parted soon after. Kelly had loved being his mother's muse, and was the source of so many paintings and drawings. When he started becoming interested in technology at eight years old, his YouTube channel exploded with people seeking their type of content, as it seemed the entire younger generation started to look for answers and found questions with them. A prolific poster of content, Kelly would show themself at their mother's classes, playing little pranks on the paying guests at the studio, and these would be interspersed with long arty walks through Central Park. They were shot in black and white mostly, as a view into the world of a small gender-fluid human finding their way in the big bad city.

Technology moved on and in the late teens Kelly was such a huge crossover star with artificially modded hormones mixing with real ones. As they approached 16, it was very publicly announced that they were transitioning back to being male, one of the first really famous influencers to do so. This served only to increase the curiosity around the story that became 'their' story as the pronouns altered. At 16, they were back to being male, thanks to a wonderful private Manhattan surgeon, paid for by the inheritance from their father, who had thrown himself out of a window of his apartment near Wall Street. Though Kelly had never had a relationship with their dad, as an only child they were the sole beneficiary of their father's estate, and once probate was granted when they turned 18, they became a very rich young individual indeed. Throw in the millions of followers across all social platforms, aside from their story, Kelly had never really worked a day in their life, which certainly was a story of note to tell!

Suki was livid. At once a modern woman but also an old-fashioned romantic, she had fallen for Kelly a few years back during a low point in her life and career. Her third album hadn't been that well received and the intensity of her schedule and her work with her cartoons was exhausting. A lot of time in California with Apple working on the world's new hit animation meant she spent a lot of time in LA, and that's where she had met Kelly, whose gravitas and instant energy was something she was perhaps looking for in her life, which had become too managed, too controlled. He was the right amount of crazy, but also the right amount of cool, and while his back story did concern her a little, he was oh so gorgeous, they made a great couple, and she could have fun with him. You could say he brought her out of her shell.

But tampering with her drink… Well, that was another story. It was a shit trick and she was pissed off that he had been a dick on her big day. Her last concert. Was she doing the right thing? She wanted a family more than anything, hers now long gone and a distant memory. She remembered her mother: a tall Japanese lady, very elegant, who was born to a dashing corporate salesman and Suki's Singaporean grandmother. Suki herself was born and raised in Singapore during a happy marriage between her mother and her Dutch father, an ex-pat businessman, who had settled there in the early 2000s back when big business was booming in Singapore and companies were scrambling to establish regional hubs in the safe and clean city state. They'd lived in a little house out in Simei, a comfortable suburb not far from the airport, and not far from the city centre either, such were the amazing public transport links that the nation was famous for. She'd attended a great school in her area that had really pushed her, but her love of performing and of the arts, coupled with her sheer majestic beauty, even as a little girl, meant she was always surely destined for stardom if her talents were nurtured. She'd been given great genetics after all with the combination of sharp dark Japanese features and a softening of the north Asian hard looks by her Singaporean grandmother. The height genetics she surely got from her handsome father, once six feet six with a striking blonde mullet, reduced to the most amazing white shock in his later years when he continued to be dashing. Her father's job meant he was away quite a lot, but the flip side of this great salary meant that Suki was encouraged into attending drama and art school, and it wasn't long before she was making a name for herself all across Singapore.

Happy times before the crash, the day that had shattered her world. On Thursday 19 November

2026, the early Christmas rains turned the ECP into a flood that her parents couldn't survive when they were hit simultaneously by a minivan and a skidding saloon coming the other way. It flipped the flower beds in the central reservation and hit them head on. Suki was 19 and her world came crashing down.

Throwing herself into her studies and staying close to her aunties and uncles on both sides, her childhood tragedy perhaps explained how she could be as deep as the ocean and why she longed for a family of her own. She wanted to replicate the magical setting she'd had with her parents, whom she loved. And they had loved each other equally as much.

If Kelly was going to do this to her now, would he ever change? His cheeky persona was great while touring and partying and everything that came with that, but could he change enough to help take care of the kids? Of her? Would he mature? She'd long worried that he had too many skeletons in his closet. I mean, changing gender was such a big thing, right? But to do it essentially four times and transition back to the gender you were born with in the first place? Surely there were things in there, deep mental health things that she hadn't seen yet, and she worried for the consequences. Was she doing the right thing?

The warmth of the bath was mirrored by the warmth within her, and she gasped as she caught the side of her nipple as she gently rubbed her sponge down her body. Neglecting her instincts—and the drugs were giving her a strong need—she furrowed her brow once again as she cursed Kelly for his faux pas and she stood up to begin getting ready for her big night.

The brown halo of the Barclays Center came into view as the Tesla expertly manoeuvred around the latecomers and stragglers of the crowd and towards the back entrance. Suki looked incredible as she exited the car, helped out by Kelly, her silver ensemble shimmering in the light breeze, long skirt and matching nearly there boob tube reflecting the light onto her impossible straight blonde locks. The six inches built into the bottom of her silver platforms elongated her frame, making her perfection seem ever more impossible.

Time for action.

She never liked to do the dressing room and rider thing, rather preferring to arrive last minute and get straight into it.

Striding onto stage, the arena was packed, the atmosphere electric, and the noise ready to greet their hero as the screens kicked in to show hero-worshipping imagery up in the sky, on screens above, screens on the stage and screens on the walls. The sensory overload was dramatic, giving the crowd the sensation that they weren't just seeing Suki, they *were* her: with her, near her, smelling her, touching her.

The sound bursts kicked in: drums, which became louder and louder, adding to the dramatisation of the show. The audience was enthralled by the globe's biggest female star, her beauty, her familiarity, her excellence.

They were in a frenzy now and cries of 'Dreamer' echoed around the inner walls as the engineered acoustics of the premium venue did their magic and amplified each and every sound, making it almost religious in its glory.

Brighter and brighter became the lights with thousands of screaming fans touching their temples to make sure their GGlasses recorded exactly the right spot. Their feeds were being played back on the screens all around them as the drums reached a crescendo and the guitar kicked in, followed by her voice…

'Well, hello New York! Are you OK?'

Silence. Black.

Shrieks.

9 The Concert: Prologue

The pool was no more than 10 lengths really—a token gesture to the health-obsessed planet—in the most basic of hotels. The whirr of the spinning bikes meshed against the soft splash of the front crawl—not that Dylan could hear anything, or even *think* anything other than his plan. There was only his plan. And he would be with her tonight. Beating off the jet lag was going to be critical if he was going to carry out his plan. The mini assistant in his room at the Holiday Inn on Schermerhorn had recommended 32 minutes of medium intensity swimming followed by a light lunch and exactly 1.2 litres of water in the 30 minutes following his leisure time.

His plan was going well so far. He had picked up his F-150 for cash and had it modded from the contact he'd made—also for cash—and he was ready to move into action. He'd already made a couple of reccies of the Barclays Center and had his outfits from one of the few in-person Targets that existed in the city. And various ID forms had all been procured and printed at the 3-D shop over the road.

Despite the lack of windows in the soulless afterthought of a hotel room, the screens still flickered and tickered away, *CNN* excitedly having crews in front of the Barclays Center, awaiting the final performance by his one true love. She was retiring to have a family, though what she didn't know was that that would be with Dylan. She'd come round, he'd make her safe, they'd go... away.

A black look took over Dylan's face as he thought about all the things he hated in this world: the boredom, the clean sanitisation of the bourgeois, how everything was seemingly predetermined, no risk, no pain, just a long slow trundle towards the mega-age. Though his mother had work—she had jobs—they were no more than barely comfortable in London. And it wasn't like he had to be out with the nightcrawlers after 02.00 in Soho. He'd never been in trouble, never arrested. He had all the money he could wish for, which turned out to be a valuable commodity when he had paid for The Book when he'd originally simply been looking to test his considerable coding prowess to see what he could do.

The GoogleCab... That had been fun: just a little four-way traffic light malfunction and a small crash. It proved he could get in there, do what he needed to, and get out again. No one came to his door, did they? Of course, they didn't! Who knew better than Dylan how to cover tracks and become invisible.

The Singapore MRT was another thrill. He wanted to be in that town. He wanted to be with her and his jealous rage saw him hack the trains, making it difficult for everyone to be where he wanted to be.

When he heard that night that she was betrothed, retiring, and that worm Kelly was revealed to be The One for her, well, that was it. That wasn't acceptable. And that was the night his plan came fully to fruition.

Rested, and his body working overdrive to combat the time zones, he had a myriad of thoughts. His teenage hormonal angst and love for Suki was palpable, and this was coupled with his hatred for the inequality of the world, which was also an overarching theme of his malaise. He longed for the distant memories of his Uncle Bradley in Canada, the seaside times when he could eat chips and still be petrified of seagulls but wouldn't be punished. His plan was conceived so as to give him what he'd always wanted in the world. But he couldn't work out how to do that properly. He was taking a massive short cut, but he reckoned that the resulting fallout from the global meltdown that was coming would buy him time with Suki, and she would grow to love him and view him as her saviour.

His EMP simulator—a third generation Marx generator—sat on the bed, the soft white linen a cushion for the metal and wires, the box powerful enough to take out an entire block. It would cause a small explosion and deliver some limited localised damage, but fused electrical wires, scrambled servers and a complete and utter malfunction of anything electrical on the entire block, *that* was the plan to get her out of there. Away from *him*. She would, in time, see that Dylan was her saviour and fall in love with him over the joys of nature and the real world in his hideout while the rest of the world imploded.

'One last SIM check,' he said to himself as he booted a screen to show the timing and sequence: from EMP firing, to grabbing the girl, to the carefully prepped sequence of lights allowing him just through at legal speeds and then shutting behind him, which would make a tail impossible and his getaway so, so easy. He'd run the calcs a thousand times, aggregating the data and coding the outcomes so that his speed and approach time to every single light was predicted to the nearest second, provided he stayed calm. And his vanilla F-150 ensured he wouldn't stand out on his trip north. It would drive for him in any case, his cargo comfortable in the modded back seat entryway to the tail, so all he had to do was sit calm until they reached the destination 13 hours and 26 minutes later.

Joe had a purpose. Level 2 was all he'd dreamed of and more: all city and action and keeping things calm. The 'Summer of Strife' was showing no signs of slowing with more tropical storms in random cities at random times. It was as if the usual hurricane season had just decided to up sticks and cause havoc somewhere else. At the slightly wrong time of year.

Tonight, he had been put on patrol around some huge concert, a nice piece of skirt alright, but the music wasn't his thing. Retro old school rock was way more satisfying than this over-the-top posturing by a plastic creature who just tried to bait her fans into her entangled world of garish outfits, loud techno-pop, social media and cartoons for all ages. Oh yeah, and the tits and ass for the daddies was a critical part too.

Joe had earned praise from General Adams for his role in calming the riots all along Fifth and down as far as Wall Street, and his work with the experimental bots had drawn him plaudits from everyone in his command. Stokes was also revelling in the applause, and Adams and Robinson were staying on and deploying the bots in more mundane settings. And what a perfect way to demonstrate peaceful law and order control than at a pop concert? Joe and Stokes had also been asked to stay on and assist in the crowd control planning with a few bots who had been dumbed down from the heavy artillery and they cut a fresher step with pistols instead of machine guns and even caps, trying to make them blend and look like human cops—only ones you would never mess with in a million years.

Though there hadn't been a specific car or traffic light failure for a few days now, tensions were still running high. However, public sentiment was beginning to turn as President Obama ran another surge of popularity for the way she held the situation, her ability as an orator perhaps only matched by her recently departed husband. The chatter on X-App was incredible with all sorts of conspiracy theories emerging as to who was behind the endless storms in both hemispheres, and who had hacked the stock market, and why were the gazillionaires all profiting from this maelstrom?

The far right crazies in the other camp were hypothesising about why the transport infrastructure seemed to be failing, and suspicion fell towards the Chinese, who were always under suspicion from someone. China had flip-flopped in its foreign policy for decades, being still a highly secretive and controlled police state, but at various times it had cosied up to Putin and rebelled against him when it appeared the whole world thought that was the right thing to do. Their economy was roaring with their well-timed abandonment of the restrictive child policies, which at various times in history had been limited to one, two and then three children. Since the late twenties they had abandoned any limit altogether, almost certainly in response to the falling fertility rates in the West that was decimating countries and economies. They had long courted Taiwan, but despite a few skirmishes that were played down in the early to mid-twenties, they had refrained from taking it. Though the whole world knew it was just a matter of time and opportunity before they would surely strike.

The evening dusk still shot light beams over the brown halo, like some sort of hat with a hole, and Joe called Monica again for a sit rep.

'You there, hey.'

'Yes.' Monica was curt, pleased to be away, but confused. Was Joe playing a game? Josh wasn't happy in the slightest that she and Benji had just upped and left, so here she was, torn between these two guys, her old love and now her annoying ex in the red corner versus her current friend-who-was-a-bit-more-than-that in the blue. Why was Joe in the red corner?

'Can you hear me? It doesn't sound like you are there.'

'Yes!' This time with more energy so Joe knew she was present but was still pissed off.

'I'm at the Barclays Center tonight. Some concert thing. Everything's still on high alert here, but it seems quieter, you know. Maybe I was a little hasty sending you away. How's my big guy?'

'Alright.'

'Can I speak to him then?'

'Just missed him. He's sleeping. And I'm having trouble explaining to him what is going on, Joe. I'm going to make arrangements to get back to NYC tomorrow.'

'OK, fine. I can't argue. Maybe I was just a little spooked by the accident and the riots and the storms… Something's not right, Monica. I can sense it.'

'Something's not been right with you for a while, Joe,' she snapped, exiting the call.

Irritated, Joe continued to scan the street. Everything normal, save for a few bots here and there as an added precaution in the 'Summer of Strife'. *CNN* analysts were wailing about the highs and lows of the stock market, general panicked tones as people were losing money hand over fist in seemingly safe stocks, yet old school infrastructure commodities were gaining strongly as the world wanted the safety of the manual solution. If you'd put all your money into gold barely two weeks before, you'd be looking at a handsome return in a short space of time.

'Jones, sit rep, please. How's the traffic out the front?' The familiar voice of Stokes in his rig boomed loudly into the gentle early evening dusk. Joe was having a blast doing real work and he enjoyed the fact that he was like a soccer coach or a controller, with these kick-ass androids who would never argue, never disobey orders, and who—he was sure—could rip a man's head off in seconds should they be ordered to. He felt young again, like it was 2019 or some long-forgotten day when the sun seemed to shine a lot and people were free. Stokes' words snapped him out of his wistful enjoyment of the early evening.

'All clear, sir. Corner of Flatbush and Atlantic all calm, sir. I have bots G7 and G8 checking the east–west flow and the south route down towards Prospect Park. No incidents, sir. All clear.'

'Good work, Jones. Same situation here on the other side. I've got H4 and R23 covering the corner of Atlantic and Sixth. All clear. Check in again, five minutes. Over.'

When on earth did anyone said 'over' anymore? Joe could not even remember where that came from, but he had just a vague recollection of old radio tech that was so glitchy and manual that each participant in such a conversation had to be very clear when they'd finished speaking. The always-connected rigs and GGlasses of today never missed a trick, and with the advancement of 6G and wireless-over-the-air recharge, nothing ever went out or lost power either as any peripheral you wanted to have or carry would always ensure it had a source. This was provided that the one weakness in the system—the lithium battery— was of good health and status.

Crossing the street to the large open expanse in front of the venue, Joe's route towards the entrance doors was disturbed by a recently familiar sound: crashing, more noise, smoke. Feelings of confusion swept over him as he ran instinctively towards the source. High in the sky the plume was coming from behind the venue. It was time to sprint. Real adrenalin and a fight or flight reaction were kicking in making him feel alive!

'Jones, here. Sit rep, please. Current location front and centre on Atlantic at Barclays. Come in, please.'

Nothing. Silence. Smoke.

10 She's Gone!

Loading the van, Dylan had made every effort to be Mr Grey. His back story was impressive: ID of the air-con engineer who had to fix a quick call-out. He'd hacked the list of approved vendors for the Barclays Center and then hacked the air-con company themselves, picking out a current engineer to be his masquerade, Renato William Sanchez, an air-con lackey who actually was on call that night, should anyone be bothered to check.

Slipping into the trade lane behind the centre, his EMP had been nicely disguised in a Brooklyn Cool packing box, heavy but manageable, and his target was an unguarded fuse spur box, nicely beside an emergency exit that led into the back halls of the venue, not far from the dressing rooms and the stage. Manoeuvring the cool box into position, he opened the lid a half crack and pulled out a long wire. Then, swiftly with his other hand, the screwdriver came out and he was into the panel in seconds, the wire finding a new home where it could deliver its charge to cause the maximum damage possible. Its eventual payload of high voltage pulses would flow through the fuse spur and into everything connected, wireless or otherwise, and make its way to the main grid. The sheer force of the contrasting energy would be enough to shred everything within a certain radius, rendering immobile anything that depended on connectivity or electricity.

'Evening.'

Dylan's heart jumped off the tallest building and was in freefall. By his calculations there was to be no one around in this area at this time, least of all another tradesman with a set of tools.

The guy with the lanyard disappeared into the service entrance and Dylan wedged his foot to catch the door as he did a slow half turn to move his head and eyes into a position, any position, in order to see where the intruder had gone.

His heart landed on the softest, most fluffy pillow imaginable as the toolman took a sharp right into the basement corridor. He probably really was an AC rigger coming to check and make sure everything was efficient while the Center was under max people load and full of heat.

Checking his small hand remote, he pulled his cap down, its rim shielding his face, as he moved slowly inside the venue, and took up his position at the left stage door.

It was just past 20.50 now and he reckoned she'd be on stage by 21.00. She was in nearly all of her concerts and was usually done before 23.00 to ensure there was no backlash from the very broad range of fans, especially the parents needing that early finish to make sure their precious little ones were safe and well rested. God forbid anyone might suffer from lack of sleep nowadays!

His analysis of Suki's concert roll, all 197 live concerts she had performed globally over the last decade, threw up an unusual statistic. There was a near 90 per cent probability that in the first two minutes of her set Suki would be at the left half of the stage. Details were crucial to Dylan. Timing was everything and he'd have less than 5 seconds and 15 paces to grab her and exit the stage, with another 15 seconds and 25 paces to be at the emergency exit, blanket covering Suki so if anyone did clock him, it would look like he was carrying an explosion survivor to safety.

Except the 'explosion' was more noise and smoke than anything approaching a real bomb. An EMP took out all of the electrical items in half a block, giving him free rein to leave and pass the traffic lights freely. Well at least for the first 42 seconds before his carefully woven pattern override saw him safely through, every light going in the rest of his gigantic escape route. He'd never be stopped!

BANG!

Dylan was perfectly positioned to escape any possibility of backlash from the blast. Smoke filled the access corridor beneath the stage, and the sound of screams penetrated the night air, which he had been prepared for, his singular focus ignoring totally the panic and pleading of the voices from all directions.

Moving swiftly and silently, he counted out his steps as planned and grabbed his target, thick blanket in place and stun shot administered, just enough for 20–30 minutes of silence.

Turning, his retraced the five long strides to the stage door. Vaulting down the last step and through the door into the rear passageway, his way was illuminated in the darkness by the tracer torch mode on his lead-shielded GGlasses. The rest of the universe was in seeming blackness, save for the neon exit signs running off the newly kicked-in backup generator.

Silently, he is counting out the steps towards his target and the door…. 14, 15, 16. Ignoring the screams and the movement behind him, he could sense that everything was random, and no one was clocking him… yet.

He continued to count…22, 23, 24. He approached the door and swung it open with his right side, his body and that of his charge swerving left to sashay through as it swung wide and then closed again. By this time, he'd repeated the action down the steps towards the Ford, parked just behind the side wall so as to save it from any damage or debris from the EMP blast. Opening the side door, he bundled Suki in through the door, effortlessly pulling the panel in the seat down so he could manoeuvre her into the crawl space, which had been custom built: AC, water spout, pillows and the right level of support so his one true love could be safe while he made the getaway.

The Ford purred softly like the old cat it was, well, a cat with a fake voice box faking the silent immediacy of the launch. He was away, swiftly but not noisily or hurriedly, then he took a hard left to exit the service lane onto the exit slip. No lights. And he smiled.

Joe continued his sprint towards the rear, puzzled as to why none of his colleagues were responding. His first confusion was the bot, which he found sitting on the floor like a doubled-over doll, legs at an impossible angle, jerking motions and squeaks and beeps as it tried to somehow regain... consciousness?

Throwing open the exit door, he found himself in a narrow corridor and headed towards the green neon stage sign, which apart from the red exit was the only thing lit up. Hurdling the side stairs in almost total darkness, all he could hear were screams of people moving wildly like a colony of ants: random, switches of direction, bumping, confusion, panic.

The smoke was starting to thin out now. It was metallic and very sharp, and it was clear there was no fire per se. Turning his head frantically in all directions as he kept his cap over his mouth to filter the air, he was almost rugby tackled by a distraught Kelly.

'Have you seen her? Suki. She's gone. Where *is* she?' he repeated when Joe struggled at first to comprehend what was being said.

'Calm down, sir. I'm trying to assess the situation. Who are you and what do you mean 'she's gone'?'

'I'm Kelly, her fiancé,' he said indignantly. 'The explosion happened, the power just went out and she's... she's *gone!*'

'Follow me, sir,' said Joe with all the politeness of his Level 3 status, coupled with just a hint of panic that this clear Level 1 situation demanded.

All around them people staggered to their feet, trying desperately to regain their senses and their hearing as the large electrical pulse had rendered a huge shock through the building.

No comms. Radio silence.

'Stokes, over here.' Joe spotted his friend and boss scrambling to his feet down near the lower exit door, helping to hold open the door as the ants escaped from the colony and headed towards whatever their mission was.

'Joe! Thank God you're alright. What's happened? Are you OK?'

'Never mind him, where is Suki?' interrupted Kelly as the three of them instinctively followed the rest of the ants towards the light, their senses and hearing coming back slowly to normal levels.

'Let's meet at the e-vac point, GCab pick-up zone 1, over there.'

Stokes led the way with an athletic push from his thighs, his Level 1 training kicking in as he took charge—as he should—Joe grabbing Kelly and pushing him through the throng in the same direction. There were others already there.

Kelly again was hysterical. 'Where *is* she?'

'Cut it out,' commanded Joe as he took human charge of someone clearly not used to trauma or incidents or even basic separation. 'Now, what did you see?'

'I didn't see anything. I saw her on stage, I heard the bang and I just kind of hit the floor. When I looked up, she was gone.'

'Jones, Davis, rear stage door. Keep a line-of-sight chain. Go! Now! Report back in 60 seconds.'

Stokes was in full-on Level 1 mode now, moving other units to the front door to help with the exit flow. 'What did you see, Joe?'

'Nothing, sir. I heard the bang as I was out front and saw the smoke coming from the rear, so I ran around into the service corridor and onto the stage. That's when I ran into... this guy.' He gestured to Kelly as if he was unsure what he was: part over-the-top styled hair and metallic clothing, part faux celebrity, who just seemed a little... pathetic.

'The bots are down, sir. Shaken up real bad. Looks like they have some auxiliary power, but it's not coordinating in their movements. And grid power is out. Repeat, no power. Can't see anything up in the immediate vicinity, sir.'

'Stokes! What's going on?' The unmistakable figure of General Adams came rushing towards the GCab stand, his sidekick Robinson in tow a half step behind.

'Unknown, sir. Explosion that doesn't seem to have caused physical damage. No electricity anywhere. Possible missing person. Sir, who is the VIP—?'

'She's GONE!' interrupted Kelly, who was met by a raised hand as Adams moved closer to Stokes to continue the debrief.

Joe calmly moved him a half step out of the way, all the while wondering how and why Adams had got there so quickly in the first place. Conspiracy theories had started the wild journey of running riot in his head and he was incapable of rational thought in a linear way due to the chaos.

'We need some comms, Stokes. I want eyes on. Where are they? They should have us up by now,' boomed

Adams, as Robinson nervously circled, unsure of whether to contribute or to stay silent and let her boss handle things.

'Yes, sir. Jones, head to the cross-section and see if you can find the e-comms team. They should be here any—'

Before he could finish his sentence, Joe had turned and moved, instinct kicking in to know what was needed. A formal wave of the arm from Kelly to Robinson told her that she had charge of this guy now.

The e-comms guy was unmistakable, the van screeching to a halt with the visible red logo, part Red Cross, part huge mobile device. One thing that was unacceptable in a battlefield these days was comms being down, so these guys had all the kit needed to make a pretty powerful hotspot mobile just about anywhere. Mobile power: G6 low latency comms fields allowing long-range hook-ups to secure systems all over the planet, tablets being dished out to the soldiers to get them back on line and talking to each other.

The professionalism of movement was stunning to watch. Joe was doing his bit to merely connect person a with person b and guide the e-comms guys to the e-vac zone, Flashing lights were coming back online in the GCab shelter and a myriad voices were booming around the comms channels as everyone established the normal chain of command.

The bot stood up, looked down at it legs as if it were about to exclaim 'sheesh' and ran its hands down its body as if it was dusting itself off, only it didn't, but you could tell that metaphorically it was.

Just then Kelly made a dash, shrugging off Robinson's pathetic attempt to grab his arm and restrain him, due to her distraction at trying to work out the rest of the events, all the while alert for any command from Adams.

The band!

You could tell it was the band, because who else would dress like that! Joe watched as Kelly sank into the six arms like a bereaved widow being told her only child was dead. He could see panic on the other three faces as they all confirmed that no, none of them had seen Suki.

11 Find Her

Darkness.

The groggy effects of the stun shot were starting to wear off and Suki was conscious first of her rigid clothing tight against her skin then of the soft cotton of the pillow. The pillow? She could hear the engine. The soft bumping every now and again told her that she was moving in a vehicle. Her compartment was no more than six feet long, four feet wide and a few feet tall. She couldn't really move but could turn over to examine for more clues as to her predicament. The hard metallic edges on the outer side of her skirt hooked her skin as she rolled 180° onto her front and shrugged off the thick blanket to one side of the compartment.

Dylan tugged again at his cap, the angle becoming ever more vertical over his nose with each passing alteration. No doubt he was subconsciously trying to hide his face. He smiled as another light turned from red to green just in time for him to roll right through at the speed limit of 60 mph. The sign for 678 Whitestone Bridge came into view. Another 10 clicks, which meant in about 11 minutes he'd be over the other side heading north to north-east. His plan was working perfectly 37 minutes in, and he'd even passed a patrol car somewhere through Williamsburg that made him pull again at his cap. But smoothly changing lanes and passing the light that moved to red the second he got through delayed any chance the trooper had of getting eyes on him, and he continued on to the next light with a smile. The smile was all faked confidence as inside his internal organs were travelling way past the speed of sound. The rollercoaster train that was his plan was well underway now and was unable to be stopped.

'Hey, HELP!'

Dylan winced as he heard the sounds. Checking his watch, he was now plus 38 minutes, and the stun shot had worked a little longer than he had calculated. No matter, he had planned for the eventuality, and would be administering another one very soon via the hand-operated rig he had built into his coffin-style trap. However, his absolute plan was for Suki to get out very much alive.

'Please be quiet. You are safe…. if you stay quiet.'

'HELP!'

'That's not quiet now, is it? Now stay *quiet*!' His calm tone remained as he ended the sentence with a menacing flourish and the cab was once again filled with the gentle hum of the tyres on the road below.

'Good.' He paused to ensure she would indeed carry out his wishes.

Silence.

'You are safe. We are going on a long journey. When we arrive at our destination, I will tell you everything. Until then, please relax and get some sleep. You will feel groggy for a time due to the stun shot I gave you for your safety.'

Suki's eyes were wide open now, and they were starting to adjust to the pitch black. She could make out the pillow, the blanket, and the weird straw that stuck into the cabin at the side of the pillow, which she tugged at, getting a wet hand for her efforts.

'Do you understand?'

'No,' she whimpered, turning once again 180° to see if there was an escape from her nightmare.

'You are safe. You are healthy and well. And you are... loved. Here, take some water,' he said, tapping the seat beside him to his right where the water bottle was propped. The straw was barely visible now as it passed through the leather near the pillow and into the carefully designed protection chamber. She knew what that was for.

'We have about 13 hours still to go. I won't be stopping. So please sip, but don't take too much as we can't stop for...' He left the unspoken word unsaid, as if it were obvious. And it was.

Suki turned again another 180°, frightened, helpless, confused, groggy... tired.

Wherever she was going, she could do nothing about it, so she figured it best to rest and see what came her way. Was she going to die? Did someone want her for money? She'd been the victim a few times of attempts to distort reality, disrupt her world, and had people seek money from her. There had been the incident in Sydney with the cleaners where they'd been looking after her suite in the Park Hyatt and had over the course of two weeks stolen numerous small but sentimental items. Then they'd taken pictures, pictures of her and Kelly together, and threatened to leak them to the press and demanded compensation for the return of her trinkets and smaller pieces of jewellery as well as the master copies of the pictures, which would not then be leaked online. Her team had sorted that and kept it out of the press for sure. She didn't care about the money.

The other time, she'd been blackmailed by her long-time housekeeper in LA, around the time she'd got with Kelly and had been partying perhaps too much. Lax security and a few unsavoury incidents with the wrong sorts of people in her life were getting out of hand and another request had come in for a large sum of money to keep quiet. Again, her team had sorted it, Bob being an absolute superstar. This one had hurt Suki as she had had a bond with Sasha, and it only fuelled her depression at the time. It took Kelly to bring her out of it: slowly, gently at first before she did genuinely fall for his sense of humour and kindness. After all, he didn't need her money, and all that stuff in the past with him switching and playing to the clicks was over now, and they were in love, and they were going to start a family.

As she thought of this, her stomach tightened and she felt a pang of doubt. Kelly dropping her the Dialezide was a mean trick. He'd done it before. All men had as the drug quickly swept the globe and became the fastest-selling drug ever. Combine a dose of that with the new turbo-charged Viagra they'd found in the early thirties and you really were in for a good night, whether you were a giver or a taker.

Just then she heard a thud on the side of her coffin-styled cell and felt a scratch: sharp, as the needle pierced her skin and lodged in her side.

'What's that? Help me, please. Please. I'll give you anything you want: money, anything. What *do* you want?'

Silence.

So tired.

Dylan smiled as she started to quieten and he realised his next dose of stun shot had worked. This one was important, a treble shot, as he needed to keep Suki unconscious and quiet until he got past his biggest threat, the Canadian border. He knew the route up would be easy, and the upgraded battery pack he'd insisted on before buying the van was coming good. He didn't even need to stop to charge. He reckoned he could get all the way to Lunenburg and his late Uncle Bradley's place.

He'd strategised that as long as no one had found him—and how could they—then the border was his only big chance of being caught. He had hidden the person concealment panel well—they could not see it if they checked the back seat—and the way he'd cladded the top of the external piece that ran into the back of the truck meant it was also disguised. It just looked like someone had modded a huge battery upgrade in there. Which they had, of course. But not there. As long as he kept to the speed limit and just blended in, he'd be good. And of course his fake British passport would never flag up on the border system and he could just sail through to the other side, away from the US, which was going to literally explode soon anyway.

The command bus roared around the corner and positioned itself just past the GCab rank. Adams beckoned Robinson and Stokes to follow him aboard, searching around for others, it seemed, before fixing his eyes on Joe.

'You. You too.'

'Jones, sir. At your service'

The inside was a purpose-built HQ: all screens, desks and people analysing endless streams of information. The command zone was an old-fashioned mahogany desk and wall unit, obviously chosen due to the general's own personal taste, which juxtaposed wildly with the modern, sleek, screened office set.

'Sit rep,' boomed Adams as Stokes took a pace forward.

'Looks like an EMP bomb was detonated to the rear, sir. Electro-magnetic pulse bomb, high grade. Extensive electrical damage for at least a block incapacitating the bots and killing the power everywhere. American Power and Gas say we will be partially restored in a couple of hours, to the exterior areas at least. It will take some time to assess the physical damage in the centre itself, sir.'

'Confirmed missing person, sir. One Suki Yakamoto who was the star of the sh—'

'I know who she is, Stokes. Get on with it,' boomed Adams again impatiently as Stokes shuffled his feet nervously to continue as if he'd just been reprimanded by the headmaster.

'Confirmed missing, sir. Robinson is working with her fiancé and the band to establish what they saw, but details are sketchy at best, sir. CCTV feeds were knocked out by the EMP, so we are struggling to determine any comings or goings.'

'What else?'

'I've spun up a command force, sir. We are programming all the capable recognition cameras across the state to alert us if we find her, and we are now checking internally all the records of sign-ins at the event. We're cross-checking lists of concert attendees and pulling the GGlass feeds and the social pictures to see what we can see *before* the EMP hit.'

Robinson chimed in, no doubt eager to impress. 'Stokes, work with Jones here and Alpha Group to double-check everyone who was employed at this event. Assign Beta Group over to the back of the bus to check the confirmed attendees and what they saw.'

'Right, get to work everyone,' interrupted Adams so they could all be clear who was really in charge as he retreated to his Chesterfield sofa, all the while gesturing wildly to program his screens 'just so' to get the updates in the format he wanted.

Joe noticed the civilian nature of Adam's suit and grabbed Stokes by the shoulder just as they were out of earshot while they moved through the bus.

'Why's he here, anyhow? Date?' He winked, nodding in the direction of Robinson, her suit equally as smart as Adam's but equally as civilian, his conspiracy theory that they weren't here for work. Stokes shrugged him off and headed for Beta Group to assign a CO for that project.

Joe moved towards the overhead sign reading 'A' above a long glass table surrounded by a few bespectacled nerds rocking the latest GGlasses. One of them instinctively stood and approached him. Clearly the leader of the geeks.

'Good day, sir. I'm Ethan, Alpha Team Lead,' he said in an impeccable Queen's English accent. This made Joe smirk. He thought of those countless drab TV shows over the years portraying the excellence of the British monarchy over time. That model of governance and historical upkeep faded into history now, save for King William, one of the last rulers of any sort of empire around the globe.

'I'm certainly no 'sir', Ethan, but it's nice to meet you. I was outside in the street with a few bots before this thing went up, so I guess they've asked me to help.'

'Well, we certainly need all the help we can, sir, and I will be your chief analyst in Alpha Team. I'll coordinate for you with the rest of the team about anything else you need.'

Joe was still in part shock, part in the zone as the gravity of the situation, coupled with the excitement of the 'real' work, energised him, yet he was bewildered to find himself in some sort of futuristic battle bus. Screens were everywhere and people were having conversations with seemingly everyone at once via the ubiquitous rigs, which made it hard to concentrate, and Joe was trying to get his head around the brief of finding out who had been there at the event on a contractual basis. Were there any workers who had seen something? Were any rigs detected in the stage area or close to backstage where they could pull some footage?

'Righto, we've got two lists for you, sir,' said Ethan in his cut glass Queen's English, hands gesturing wildly as the banks of screens in front of him exploded with data.

'List one: 14 names—this is from the Beta team—confirmed people at the event with criminal records.' The first screen whirred into life like the world's fastest PowerPoint show, displaying a mug shot of all 14 and the crimes they had committed, each for a second before repeat.

'This one is interesting. German Castro. Served five years in 2025 for kidnap of a minor.'

'What's the other list?' said Stokes, the irritation in his voice barely disguised as if he didn't like this list at all. Call it intuition, but he didn't like the notion of lightning striking twice.

'List two is anyone detected by the system today who was here within four hours of the gig and who has a criminal record. Alarmingly, sir, 47 people! We've ranked them in order of severity of their crimes. It includes a released double murderer from 1992.'

'Yeah, that makes him 68. He'd have to be in major shape to plan this. Too efficient.'

Joe was looking down, trying to contain his frustration at the data, all the while racking his brain as to who could have done this, and why.

'Ethan, where are you from? And how old are you?'

'Sudbury-on-Thames, sir. London. I'm 27. Graduated from Oxford with first class honours, sir. I've been schooled by the MOD in the UK and I'm now on secondment to the FBI. Sir.'

'And here's me thinking you were fresh out of school and hadn't even kissed a girl yet.' Joe was visibly irritated and lashing out.

'Well, sir, there was once a blonde called Gemma down by the river, but my statistical analysis of her social media meant I knew it wouldn't last. She liked cats.'

'For sure the only chance of pussy you ever gonna get, Ethan. Now get me something else 'cos this is a load of bullshit. We're looking for something sophisticated here. People don't just rock up with EMPs by accident. Someone *planned* this.'

12 Near Miss

'Benji, come on, we're going to be late,' barked Monica as she waited for the GCab to arrive.

She'd managed to get them a flight from Philly to NYC that evening. As much as Joe's family were lovely people, she couldn't wait to get home, and to normality, if that was even possible in this crazy summer.

Your GCab will be here in four minutes, Monica,' spoke the ever so polite HIM that controlled the old-fashioned farmhouse, and Monica moved quickly over to Benji to help him stuff the last of his clothes into the bag.

'But mom, why the rush? Can't we stay here a little longer? Daddy might come here to see us.'

'Your daddy is busy, Benji. There's stuff going on and he has a new job now. He has to make sure people are safe, sweetie. We'll see him faster if we get home,' lied Monica. Anything to placate him and soothe his angst.

In today's ubersafe world it wasn't easy to be a child of a broken home. With the rise in demand for mental health support, couples' counselling and marriage support, the good old American notion of the family had surged in popularity in the thirties, divorce rates tumbling in complete juxtaposition of the suicide rates. It seemed that mental health coaching was always successful—just in one final way or the other. Relief, change and true help, or a spiral into a realisation that change wasn't possible, and the ultimate way out. The Government tried to step in by introducing measures such as the three-day week to give more people jobs and a purpose and by heavily subsidising family activities and 'fun stuff'. Even that couldn't save some people. Controversy raged over what should be done.

Bright sunshine greeted them as they stepped out onto the veranda. Waving goodbye, they were greeted by their metallic chauffeur on the side of the vehicle, facial recognition opening the doors with a swoosh and even popping the boot open for the cases. Only it couldn't yet lift them in for you!

'No music,' ordered Monica before the GCab started its monologue.

'Destination is Philadelphia Airport, Terminal One, United Airlines. Journey time will be 28 minutes. Outside temperature is 98°. However, in accordance with your saved preferences, I have set the internal temperature to 72°.'

'Yes, confirmed,' interrupted Monica before the cab could ask permission.

'Fasten your seat belts please, and our journey will begin.'

The bright sunlight was obvious but not uncomfortable thanks to the auto shields on the GCab removing the glare. Farmland rolled past as the smooth electric drive train shifted through imaginary gears and propelled them to their destination. A quick one-hour hop to NYC and then they'd be home. Sure the traffic would be rotten with the road closures and the curfews in place, but they'd be home.

What had Joe been thinking sending us away like that? she thought to herself. Monica was still unsettled, torn between her old love for her husband and wanting to stretch out for a new life, one where Benji could grow and develop and realise a great education. And one where she could be... loved.

'Mom, can I ask the G to play my Minecraft Battle, please?'

'Well, seeing as you've asked so nicely, go on then.'

'G, please call up my last saved game on Minecraft Battle.' His little voice sounded weird talking to a car, but he was indeed understood, and it was a few seconds while the cab recalled his account and asked for his mother's authorisation and confirmation code.

What looked like an old-fashioned aeroplane seat table flipped down in front of Benji, with a gaming controller inside, which he retrieved. Then he clicked his fingers towards the left-hand side screen, which he would use for his entertainment.

'Low volume please, G. I have a headache.'

'As you wish, ma'am,' replied the operating system as it flicked the number five onto the screen in front of Benji's already loading game.

The crossroads looked like something out of a history book with a train track at one side. Four-way stop signs gave way to a short crawl towards the lights, which were in place to control the train traffic that wouldn't come—not now that drones were faster and cheaper in moving goods from A to B and trains only now existed for really long-range high-capacity cargo drops. There was also the odd tourist train, but that was more for the purposes of nostalgia than anything else, being kind of like a cross between the Orient Express and the Cape Town Blue Train.

Ah, holidays... Maybe she would book one when they got back to NYC.

She remembered their last one as a family. A week in Fort Lauderdale in Florida was about all they could afford on the joint salary of a Level 3 cop and a school teacher. Never mind, in 2035 it had been an amazing time. Benji was walking and toilet training well, and he could be easily entertained with cheap Chinese plastic toys, so it was relatively easy for them to have a semblance of normality. Lazy evenings of walks along the beachfront promenade, some great chicken at Hooters, and days spent by the swimming pool at their hotel were a distant but very fond memory for Monica. They had started to find differing world views by this stage, but arguments were small and few and far between, and she remembered the feeling of hope they all had for Benji's future prospects, and of the world finally settling down after what had seemed like two decades of constant turmoil.

She'd been lost for a while during that time, her parents' car crash when she was 19 leaving her very alone and very rich, and while she wasn't a career high-flyer by any means, she enjoyed being a teacher and longed to give back to the world and her community. She'd met Joe in the mid-twenties when he'd visited her school to give a talk on community policing, and she'd loved his cheeky attitude and sense of humour. He had an energy that was enticing, and it wasn't long before one thing led to another and they were a couple. He had been the love of her life. Her comfort and security blanket of an only child without parents and all alone in the world. She wondered if they could get back what they had lost. Her colleague Josh was indeed a sympathetic ear, and she had built up so much angst in the years since the three-day week reduced everyone's life to... well, less. He'd been there for her as her anxiety built over Joe's quite obvious depression, over Benji's future, over all of their health issues, and things just seemed to spiral.

Was she regretting her decisions?

Lurching forward, her arm instinctively reached out to her left to protect Benji as the sudden halt caused him to rock forward. 'What's going on, G?' she barked to the cab as they stopped. Then she noticed the red light. Surely there couldn't be a train?

'Train incoming, ma'am. It's 68 seconds away.'

'Oh, OK,' she responded, her surprise now dissipating, and she looked left and right for sight of the cargo. Or maybe it was that tourist train.

'Mom, what's happening? Why are we stopped?' whinged Benji, his concentration on his game having been rudely interrupted by the sharp braking.

'Train, sweetie. We have to let it pass. Won't be long,' she answered as she surveyed the brown and gold landscape baked by the sun.

Waiting.

Waiting.

No train.

'G, you said "train incoming". Nothing has passed. What is happening?'

'I'm sorry, there appears to be an error. Contacting guest services for you now. One moment.'

A lady appeared on the screen where the road had been.

'Apologies, Mrs Jones, it appears there was a faulty warning light of a train. We are rebooting the light sequence now and ordering your G to move on and ignore the light. One moment.'

The car silently pulled off as G remarked, 'Continuing our journey. Arrival time 21 minutes.' And a slight rumble seemed comforting as the car ran over the tracks.

Noise. A Horn. Louder.

Monica did an about-face to pivot her neck out of the back window and saw the cargo train miss them by inches as it hurtled past at what must have been 200 mph at least. She screamed for G, demanding to know what was going on as these things didn't break, they didn't malfunction. What was happening?

Ethan looked up from his desk and seemed rather pleased with himself, like he had finally got further than that kiss with Gemma down by the river. Living alone in a Manhattan apartment wasn't easy for a young British guy these days, even one as publicly educated and privately travelled as Ethan. One of three children of a serving government minister and a public school headmistress, Ethan was a high achiever in life in academic terms. His time at Oxford had been fruitful, and then a scholarship to the Defence Academy in Shrivenham, the DCMCI building on his intellect and giving him specific skills, which he was already adept at mastering. An expert in data gathering and intelligence, he'd also studied cybersecurity and was top of his unit in graduation, landing a plumb job with the MOD and now a secondment to the FBI no less.

His private life was less secure as, coupled with his obvious lack of experience with the opposite sex, he also possessed an intelligence level that made it difficult for him to connect with ordinary people. He was polite and engaging, but it always seemed like his brain was one step ahead of other people, and even while you were speaking to him, he was three steps ahead in the conversation. His parents thought time in New York would toughen him up and give him a chance to stand on his own two feet and learn how to live a life. Yet, in practice, the solitary confinement of a strange city with people he just couldn't understand enough to talk to, people who seemed to be on a different planet to him, well, he struggled, and although he loved his job, he was fast becoming almost a hermit outside of his work.

Beckoning to Joe, it seemed he had some news.

'Well, sir, my final list is very, very interesting. We ran a list of all contractors at the event, people with access for a variety of reasons: catering staff, security, even the set-up crew for the equipment. We cross-referenced that with a list of people with criminal records—only two: a security guard and a roadie for the crew. Minor infractions it seems.' Ethan wasn't finished. 'But then, sir, I don't know why, but I did a different cross-check and it seems one contractor kind of checked in, well, twice.'

Joe's whole body suddenly changed, demeanour morphing into the alert and interested, eyes wide and bulging. This could be something.

'What do you mean "twice"?'

'Well sir, the cameras record where a person is at all times, and just before the explosion, one guy was in the basement cellar *and* he was also scanned at the back entrance near the stage.'

'Get me the details.'

Ethan gestured again with his wrist and enlarged the mug shot appearing on screen.

'Renato William Sanchez, 38, married, lives in Brooklyn, air-con engineer. He got a call to come and fix the cooling in the cellar for the main bar, arrived at 20.40, checked in via the main entrance, and was still in the basement cellar at the time of the explosion: 21.00 hours, sir. Yet at the same time, he was at the back entrance at 19.50. So, unless the camera was faulty in the basement, he couldn't be in two places at once, sir.'

'Get me everything about him. What do we know, and where is he?'

'Copy that,' said Ethan as he went into full-on conductor mode again. Information was flying up on screens all around them, including Sanchez's current location and live CCTV feed of him in his van moving away from the scene.

'Get me his music list. He have any Suki on it?'

Screens whirred again like a fast-moving roulette wheel as Ethan brought up the info with a combination of rhythmic hand movements and spoken commands. At each stage, the NYPD access override moved seamlessly through every password protocol with ease.

'One album, sir, barely played. Actually looks like it's for his daughter, sir. It's copied to her playlist where it is used—a lot.'

'Get him in.'

13 Find Him

'Joe, are you there? Can you hear me? Why are you putting me to voice?' shrieked a clearly startled Monica as she stood at the side of the road, clutching Benji's hand tightly.

'I'm helping with a case. Have to be quick. What's up?' hissed Joe back in that kind of half-whisper, half-irritated tone.

'We've, we've been in an accident, Joe. I'm scared. Maybe you were right about something "going on".'

'Slow down, slow down. What's happened? Is Benji OK?'

'I'm fine, Daddy. Hello Daddy,' chimed in Benji as he was glad of the connection to his dad.

'Yes, yes, he's fine. We were in a GCab on the way to the airport. It stopped at a red light for ages 'cos of the train and then they said it was a problem, so they moved us on. And then the train wasn't there. But, it *was* there, Joe. It nearly hit us. We are at the side of the road now. I hit the emergency button and GCabs are sending a new car. I don't know what's going on, Joe.'

'You and me both, Monica. Listen, I'm in the middle of a big case here. Can't say too much. I'll check in later. Just get to NYC and lie low, you understand? Avoid crowds.'

'OK, OK. Thanks for... understanding,' said a clearly rattled Monica, who was thankful for Joe being there, for picking up, and for being someone she could go to.

The sun baked overhead now, and both Monica and Benji drew glances from just about every vehicle that passed, the automatons transporting them never once slowing or stopping to help as they waited. It was very unusual to see people actually on the streets in the burbs, and they must have cast a funny sight for the people travelling by as they waited for the new GCab to arrive.

'Here is the route map, Monica. Your replacement vehicle will arrive in four minutes,' she was told by her rig as it beamed a map into her field of vision.

It's so hot. Hurry, she thought to herself as she held Benji's hand and they patiently waited.

'Sir, sir, I have something,' chirped Ethan as he flounced towards Joe, who was flicking the corner of his brow and ending his call with Monica.

'It's a list of all vehicles leaving the area right after the EMP exploded. Unfortunately, I have to go two blocks out to pick up the working lights in three different exit routes: 129 in the three minutes following detonation.'

Joe's eyes rolled. Visibly. Deliberately.

'Don't be like that, sir. Of course I have more. What do you take me for?'

'Don't let me answer th—' smiled Joe as he stopped himself mid-sentence. He was the new guy here after all, but he figured Ethan was a good kid and could take him busting his balls just a little every now and again.

The buzz in the air was palpable. The clicking of keyboards meshed with the frantic movement of data on screens, coupled with a formality to proceedings, no doubt brought on by having the big chiefs around.

Ethan moved towards the largest panel in the centre of the run and flicked his head at a jaunty angle to access the facial recognition. Then he proceeded to chunter super-fast commands at the screen, all the while whirling his hands like an operatic conductor, the screens cycling through maps and data at his every command.

'This could be a blind alley, but from my first list of 129, I've found three vehicles that are really interesting. Here they are.'

A trio of vehicles appeared on screen, their stock images spinning as if on their sales website, data appearing all around them.

'All three of these cars changed hands recently with no known bank transaction accompanying them.'

'Meaning cash?'

'Exactly,' purred Ethan, clearly proud of his discovery. Cash was almost non-existent now, and spending it in large amounts, although not illegal, was clearly discouraged in the everything digital age and beyond, which had started in the early twenties.

'What's even more interesting are the pictures of these cars at their last crossing points of a significant traffic routing system. Look.'

'Car 1: Tesla C20. Windows set to clear. You can see a family in this car: two children in the back.'

'Uh-huh, unlikely to be our MO,' muttered Joe, clearly unimpressed.

'Car 2: Nissan Forest 3. Two young girls, just as unlikely to be our targets, and besides, they stop just after the lights, turning into a McDonald's and they get out. Not them.'

'But Car 3, Joe, Car 3 is an F-150, double cab, rear windows set to opaque, only a single male driver in situ, hard to see as he's wearing a baseball cap, but he just doesn't stop, Joe. He doesn't stop. I can't get a good look at him, at *any* light.'

'What do you mean? Track his progress. He must get stopped further up the highway,' barked Joe back, clearly now very interested.

'Well, that's the thing, Joe, he never, ever gets stopped by a light. It's like they are all letting him through, like they've been programmed to let him through...' Ethan's eyes widened at the possibilities and the myriad of conspiracies he was only just starting to imagine. You could tell he lived his life from the endorphin kicks from his brain, not unusual in the Alpha–Beta generation born in the 2010s and the 2020s as the slow removal of civil liberties and well, fun, from any aspect of life targeted people inwards, and the easy access to information meant that learning was just so easy. People became cleverer, but more introverted, and social skills were at an absolute premium. Those that had them or could develop those skills tended to rise in organisations as they learned to manage the ubernerds and make sense of the information they could provide. Ever since the Covid crisis of the early twenties that decimated the libertarian nature of governments, the 'for your own protection' and the 'Build Back Better' mantra meant people were controlled by authoritarian police states, especially in the West. This gave rise to the Alpha and Beta generations being the ubernerds—shy, clever, thoughtful—and the millennials and Gen Zs who ran the show were able to call the shots. Joe was certainly one of those who had the people skills, and he could sense that Ethan was on to something, so rather than constrict, examine his information or methodology, it was best to cut him loose, allow him to chase after his own endorphins, and basically, get out of his way.

'Great stuff, buddy. You are some guy. Keep going. Go hunt down who the man in the cap is and let me know, OK? And another thing, Ethan, but since you haven't yet told me, I think I know the answer: what happened to the Renato Sanchez lead?'

'Dead end, sir. We've had him in. He had been *exactly* where he said he was. His ID was cloned. We're still talking to him though, so I'll let you know if anything comes of it. So sorry I didn't inform you earlier, sir, it's just, I had new leads.'

'Of course you did, buddy. Keep going, pal.'

The signs kept coming. Progress was smooth and after a while she went back to sleep, no doubt groggy still from the initial shot.

Meriden 91. Only 11.5 hours more to go, but Dylan was alert. He'd methodically planned out his sleep habits and his nutrient intake perfectly, so he was in perfect shape, at the perfect moment.

Suki was silent.

At this moment she was kind of awake, barely conscious, but aware of being alive, *glad* to be alive, but so, so scared. Sleep was indeed enticing, not only from the calm embrace of the pharmaceuticals, but the low gentle hum of the ridged asphalt was relentless, and the soft warm coverings of whatever type of box she was in was so, so soft. Who was doing this? What did they want with her? That comment about being 'loved'? What was all that about? She had to be ready for when the vehicle stopped. What was she being driven in? Too small to be a car. Didn't feel overly big like a bus. Certainly no air brakes, but then again, they hadn't stopped. Not once. She was prepped to make a big noise at any traffic lights in case they were in the city and people happened to be walking by. But they hadn't stopped. And the car speed seemed fairly constant. So, no big accelerations and hardly any braking… maybe it *was* a bus and she just hadn't heard the air brake hiss? And there wasn't *much* noise other than the road, though she swore she could hear her own music, the chorus of 'Blinded by the Light' was going through her head, and she swore she could hear it somewhere around.

Dylan spoke to the car.

'ETA, please.'

'At current average velocity, 11 hours and 28 minutes. Variable route factors include traffic density around Boston, the Canadian border crossing and some toll routes which may cause delays.'

'OK then. Now please play my personal concert with Suki: London, October 2036.'

'Here it is...'

Dylan's face appeared in the centre console screen as what appeared to be a homemade video started. With a quick flick of his brow down and to the left, a tap to the GGlasses, a flick upwards and another tap, the screen image shifted to centre right of the car's HUD, which was more or less the full right-hand side of the windscreen, with the occasional road sign or pulled-over car in the verge ghosting through the image. This was another recent innovation to improve road safety even further with the eventual goal of zero incidents still not yet being achieved, but close, as cars generally drove *you*, and their constant interaction meant that fender benders just didn't happen. The handful of accidents occurring every year were usually pilots putting the car in manual at the wrong time, and well, human error.

The video continued, with Dylan moving through the crowd excited, and the camera then panning to the stage, immediately focusing on the pneumatic blonde goddess appearing on the left-hand side of the screen, her shiny metallic dress looking like the hottest medieval knight that ever did roam! The camera continued to move through the crowd, getting closer, closer, and as the music started up, the unmistakable face came into view as she roared:

'Well, hello London! Are you OK?'

It was Suki, the bass kicking in and her head and whole body rocking right back as she belted out the first line. 'Dreamerrrrrrr…'

The concert seemed to be so real, so personal, shot uniquely from one person's perspective. Except it was unlike any 'real' home movie because of the smooth camera movement, how it panned, how it zoomed right in on the star in the exact gap between two taller people. Then there were the effortless cuts to the above-sky cameras, the perfect audio, the perfect visuals. This was for sure one of those My Concerts, a composite mash-up of self-shot material, coupled with all other available crowd-funded material and paid-for professional drone and boom shots from cameras all over the venue. These things were not cheap, but as a memento of a special time, they were priceless, and gave a unique first-person perspective. Mesmerising.

Dylan arched his neck and rounded out his shoulders, settling himself in for a good couple of hours when he knew he wouldn't hit a single problem.

14 Got Her

There is rain, and there is *rain*. Storm rain, hot tropical rain. Bouncing high off the pavement, rivers of water collecting and falling towards and down the storm drains. Water seemingly everywhere, the sky as dark and grey as the mood of many nations, all facing this unseasonal onslaught of the water. The *CNN* ticker was counting these weird instances around world, all the while moving across the bottom of the window, as Joe wakes in his unfamiliar hotel room.

'...and in Singapore we go live there as the unprecedented storms have today closed one of the main motorways, the famous ECP, or East Coast Parkway, that runs right into the centre of the city state from the airport. The sheer volume of water running along the road has made progress impossible, and yet the end of September is usually regarded as the end of the southwest monsoon season—a bit of a misnomer as although rain is common most days, September usually is in the bottom half of months in the year for overall rainfall. Precipitation levels in the last few days of the month have so far exceeded those of a normal December, and governments and climate change experts are today meeting to try and find out the cause of the problem.'

'Call Ethan.'

It was 06.05 and Joe had barely slept anyway. Monica had called from Philly to say their flight had been delayed until that morning, so he was keen to understand the overnight progress on the MISPER case. He knew that Ethan would have been awake for many hours anyway.

'Ah, good morning, sir. We have news!'

'I knew you would, Ethan. Hit me with it.'

'Well, sir, the F-150 we found yesterday is of interest for sure. It has not hit one single traffic light—anywhere. In fact, it's still going, sir. It hasn't stopped. And it's approaching the Canadian border now at St. Stephen. We have units ready to intercept. We've also got the previous car owner coming in at 08.30, sir. I thought you could help us with that interview. This is very exciting, sir, but there's more.'

'Go on.' Joe quickened his pace across to the other side of the room, his coffee now more important than ever, as he was enthralled by the very traditional Englishman and his quirks and needed to be alert.

'General Adams has the boardroom booked for 09.00, sir. The CEO of Alphabet is coming to see him. He wants you in on that, too. All of us. It seems that something weird is going on with their coding. They've got spikes of incidents with GCabs, various crossings have reported failures, and this, well, case of a vehicle travelling hundreds of miles, *hundreds*, sir, and not hitting a single light or crossing. Well, it's never been heard of, sir. It's unbelievable.'

'I'll be over in five, Ethan. Great work.'

Monica had really taken the arrival delay in her stride. Call it her mothers' instinct to be so protective, calm and cool, despite all that had happened with the GCab and the railway the day before. She'd booked a quick stop at the now ubiquitous SleepPod store at the airport, and they were at least comfortable, safe and warm. A double pod with extra soft pillows, 68°, simulated fresh air, chilled water both sides, and the optional upgrade to the deluxe screen version, which had the unfortunate side effect of being mostly occupied all night by Minecraft Battle—Benji mixing screen time between the actual game and the show, a semi prime time gaming–reality TV hybrid that *all* the kids watched, especially cool seven-year-olds like Benji.

'Come on, Benji. Let's get going. We can check at the gate to see if we're boarding soon.'

Bags grabbed, and the whoosh of the pod's gullwing door gave way to the bright light of the terminal. They both swung their legs over the side and hopped onto the hard tiles. The whizz of the pod starting up the prepping of the cleaning bots was unmistakable.

'Thank you for using the SleepPod. We hope to see you again soon.'

The airport was busy, people walking with purpose, and there seemed to be a mood in the air. Tense.

Monica tapped her glasses. 'Tell me my boarding gate and send shoe directions please.'

Her Vans buzzed as her glasses responded at a volume that only she could hear. 'Gate D14. Sending directions now.'

Her right shoe vibrated strongly as she grabbed Benji's hand and manoeuvred him to the starboard. GGlasses chimed in again:

'Notification of boarding at 08.00 with scheduled departure at 08.30, arriving 09.45 into JFK, New York. You will arrive at the gate at 06.45 under current velocity.'

'What do you want for breakfast, baby?'

'Oooh, donuts! Dunkin'!' was the obvious answer from the seven-year-old as Monica rolled her eyes.

'OK then,' she replied, hitting her frame again. 'Tell me where the Dunkin' is, please. I'll have my usual and Benji will have a sugar ring and a small OJ to go.'

'Nearby Gate B1. Sending shoe waypoint now. Order is confirmed and will be ready in six minutes. You should be there in five. Go to machine C.'

'Copy that,' Monica said as she dragged the beaming child to the port this time, narrowly avoiding a rushing lady with a trolley she could barely see over.

The omnipresent screens flickered the ticker tape news above them, to the side, left and right. There was no escaping the right now. Talk about always on. Monica sipped her coffee as she finally took notice of one particular piece of news.

'Chaos continues in downtown New York today where a police curfew is in place amid reports of continued traffic light failure in the Midtown area from Park Avenue all the way to 9th and as far south as the Empire State Building. Police cordons and bots remain in place and citizens are advised not to travel under any circumstances to the Midtown area.'

The screen shot back to the perma-tanned and perma-smiling presenters as they faked a more solemn facial expression.

'And in other news, there are still no positive reports regarding the possible abduction of the pop star known as The Asian Princess, Suki Yakamoto, who disappeared from her concert at the Barclays Center last night. Let's cross to our reporter live to find out more...'

Wasn't that the gig Joe was at last night? thought Monica to herself as she saw Benji poking his fingers into the donut, basically doing everything he could rather than just eat it.

'Come on Benji, hurry. It says we are boarding soon. Finish your donut,' she said as she dragged him starboards again, and made towards the gate.

'Mom, mom, LOOK!' screamed Benji excitedly through his last mouthful of donut as he ran towards what at first glance looked like another SleepPod. But this one was taller and not as elongated. The sign above said 'Recording Studio' and Monica clocked that it was one of the latest trends for kids where they could go in and record their own song with a pop star.

'Can I do it, Mom, can I? We have time, right?'

Rolling her eyes, Monica walked closer to the machine and tilted her head to centre the QR code in the middle of her rig. The HIM piped up in her ear with the choices of cost and time as she approved the transaction.

'Go on then,' she agreed as she pushed him gently in the middle of his back, having opened the door and grabbed his still unfinished OJ with the other hand.

'Good morning, new customer. How may I address you today?' said the studio's autobot as it started showing some of the options on the screen in front.

'I'm Benji.'

'OK... Benji, who is your favourite pop star that you'd like to record with today?'

'Suki.'

An image of the beauty appeared on the screen with her cartoon self in the lower corner, unmistakable in the silver metallic dress.

'Is this correct? Please say yes or no.'

'Yes. Can I have the song 'Dreamer'?' said Benji, perhaps a little too quickly for the controller, because it paused for a few seconds to work it out. 'Dreamer' was Suki's huge hit from 2036, number one in literally every country on the planet, which made it a true global number one. The Global Office for Statistics scraped all of the data around song plays, additions to playlists, appearances on TV, all of which made up the new charts as to what and who were most popular across many different territories. Basically, only China and North Korea were the only countries who refused to sign up.

The microphone moved towards Benji and adjusted to his height as an image of Suki and him appeared together on screen. Her images were mirroring his and she was moving expertly to the rhythm of his movements, and even mirrored how he sang. Her voice clearly filled in for the odd word that the customer missed, and tuned itself lower in pitch and volume when the client managed to get back on time and hit the right notes.

Monica stood outside, the glass door letting her view the insanity going on inside, and she smiled, as she always loved her boy having fun and enjoying himself. *A long time until he needs to worry about anything, hopefully*, she thought to herself as her heart beat faster to the entertainment filling her with love.

'Sir! Come quick.'

Joe charged towards the back of the battle bus where Ethan stood conducting the screens again as images whizzed and whirred around a plethora of slick near invisible screens.

'He's approaching the border position, sir. We've got visuals on the truck.'

The F-150 slowed as it approached the tail-end of the queue and gently took its obedient position in line.

Dylan tugged at the peak of his cap and turned the volume up a notch and tried to look bored. This was the last hurdle, his plan being executed to perfection so far, and the knowledge he'd gleaned from The Book being the master stroke. With it, he'd found the key to a number of prompts used in the Google AI that controlled the traffic lights, all down to multiple inputs regarding traffic density, weather, and even local events which determined when and how often each light was triggered to slow the other side or allow the perpendicular direction a turn. Coding his own exception was then easy with the number recognition cameras picking him up at every turn and ensuring he always had green and would never be stopped. Stopping was the risk. He couldn't control who might be in the vicinity, who could get eyes on his truck, and who might be looking for them. He was sure there would be a massive man hunt, such was Suki's popularity across the globe. But by minimising that risk, he was confident they could sail through undetected until his final problem, the Canadian border. By timing the stun shot he'd administered, he knew that Suki would still be out, perhaps not fully, but unlikely to be able to make much noise in any case. She would wake a few hours before his final safe house in Canada in a remote part of Nova Scotia, which he knew well thanks to his travel with his parents when he was a kid, and his Uncle Bradley who had lived there till he'd died of course.

All of a sudden, the power cut from the overhead gantries and the long black nozzles of the rifles moved between cars, guided by what seemed like an entire squadron of elite soldiers. Joe shouted for Stokes to come, and grasped Ethan's shoulder tightly, anxious of what could be found.

One of the soldiers flung the driver's door open and out popped a cap followed by a scrawny figure of a young man: dark hair, somewhat gothic, now face down on the asphalt with what seemed like 100 guns pointed at his head.

Other soldiers surrounded the F-150 and stormed it like ants do a hole in the ground, grabbing at seat cushions and random belongings as they desperately tried to find the girl.

Multiple bodycams were now on the screen, and the dizzying effect of trying to make sense of the myriad directions was at once somewhat nauseating, yet fascinating, and Joe instinctively locked on to something that caught his eye.

'Number 2, rear seat, down by the seat belt clasp. Looks to be a small metal loop. Does that lead to anything?'

In the other camera, soldiers bundled Dylan into a van that did not hesitate to speed off, tyres screeching as the other bodycams continued to fill all parts of the screens.

The rear seat flopped forward revealing a hidden compartment and the unmistakable shock of blonde hair right at the top of the fur-lined hideaway. Reaching in, he pulled her forwards and sat her up in the back seat.

'It's her. She's alive! Great job, everyone,' boomed Joe, as high-fives abounded in the back of the battle bus.

Suki took a sharp intake of breath, and recoiled at the black-masked figure in front of her.

She was alive.

15 Two Planes

'General Adams, lovely to meet you,' said the tall wiry figure in the immaculate suit, all confidence and aftershave as he walked in like he owned the place.

The CEO of Alphabet. Lloyd Guzman. Since the AI revolution of 2028 when Google overthrew Microsoft and allegedly stole the assets of OpenAI and Microsoft in a hostile takeover that was *the* talk of Wall Street, *CNN* and indeed the world for months, Alphabet had cemented its place as the #number one corporation on the planet with a profit and loss bigger than the GDP of most European countries. They controlled the majority of personal AI assistants, which of course was a huge recurring monthly subscription that no one could do without, and also the peripherals required to operate the assistants in the modern age. Though the glasses were very cheap at a few hundred bucks, they also owned the screen and speaker hardware, the installation services of all solutions, both commercial and domestic, and of course the patented integrations with just about every service provider on the planet to allow transactions to happen. Ordering that coffee in advance at Dunkin'? They worked with Dunkin' to make that work. Or rather, the AI farms, offshored in the cooling seas of the Arctic, did. These were floating Intelligence Farms, which were moored off the King

Christian XI and X coasts off Greenland, supercharging their economy and turning all the Scandi nations, who used their cool seas and highly skilled workforce to insource similar projects, into economic powerhouses. The sub-parts of Alphabet ran into hundreds now, Google being the most recognised still, with a myriad of others no one had even heard of.

Adams eyed the slick operator carefully as he also sat and beckoned Joe and Stokes to follow his lead.

'So, sit rep. Mr Guzman, please, just what on earth is going on?' boomed Adams as he furrowed his brow quizzically.

'Well, sir, it seems we have a grade one tear in our AI architecture. Someone has opened an impossible backdoor into our code and installed a series of prompts and malicious AI interlopers to effectively cause chaos in our interconnections, sir.'

'Go on.'

'Well, it seems that a bypass was made in the traffic light system with a newly created digital AI cousin bypassing the ethics system of our signalling codebase. This effectively ordered each light to secede from anything but green once a particular vehicle approached.'

Joe had to cut in. 'We've just stopped that vehicle at the Canadian border. It's a young British guy, who kidnapped the pop star Suki last night from Brooklyn. It must have been his escape plan.'

'Look at this,' chimed in Ethan, his cut glass accent making it sound like everyone was going to watch an Oscar-winning drama, which he'd just penned.

Whirling his hands and occasionally tapping the rim of his rig as if he had a Tourette tic, a clearly excited Ethan arched his back as his masterpiece came on the screen in front of them.

Traffic cams.

'This is the F-150. Look at it move past every single light. Every single one.'

The screen kept jerking as the mash-up of small video clips kept rolling on, the changes in camera definition and placement of the truck in each scene making it seem like an old relic from an early bit-based computer game. However, the impact of what they were seeing was clearly huge.

Guzman's eyes widened as he looked stunned, frightened even, then nervously clearing his throat, he stuttered, 'Em, where, where, is he now? We, must, I mean, *must* get to him immediately.'

Stokes cut in. 'He's on a fast chopper down here. ETA 11.00. We are decamping to Jacob K Javits right after this meeting, ready to receive the mark.'

'I *must* speak to him right away,' spluttered Guzman. 'You all have no idea of the trouble we are in.'

The others sat silent for a bit, even Adams, who was usually the #numberone alpha male taking charge of every situation like this. Guzman was genuinely spooked and his eyes darted around from person to person as he searched for more information and a way in to the problem's core. He wanted to fix it. He *had* to fix it. His VPs were freaking out and he was trying to stay as calm as he could.

Guzman had an interesting back story, if somewhat predictable. Born in Borough Park, Brooklyn, his family were orthodox Jews and steadfastly religious. Raised in a very strict environment, he was exceptionally self-disciplined. He was an alumnus of Stanford where he'd graduated with top honours and was quickly snapped up by McKinsey, his early days as a management consultant giving him a broad view of business. Then he'd left to join Alphabet in 2015, rising through the ranks to eventually become CEO in 2035. He didn't suffer fools at all, but more recently, as his workload and his job had exploded, he'd reverted to type, sometimes being disruptive and challenging people openly. He also seemed quite emotional, which belied the strict educational principles he'd always adhered to in earlier life. No matter, he was the boss and people danced to his tune, having to be quick with their answers.

'Stokes, Jones, let's get over to Javits and prep the intel room for the boy's arrival. Take Guzman with you. We will watch from obvs windows. We have to find out everything this kid has done, and fast.'

Adams spun on his heels and left abruptly, Robinson as ever a half step behind. Salutes from all directions as Robinson closed the door behind them both.

The car sped over the bridge in defence mode with the other vehicles' sirens so loud that Joe could hardly think. He was beside Stokes and Ethan in the sleek automated CyberTruck, which seemed inches from the other vehicles as it zoomed ahead of the second truck containing Adams and Robinson, and Guzman, who by now was part of the team. He'd explained that the AI cousin that had been programmed into the traffic lights system and coinfected the trains, could potentially spread to all other DOT—Department of Transportation—sectors, including the plane network all across the US and even further. The AI was self-replicating and had been programmed to bypass a number of altruistic safety nets that were there to protect the system and the user. By fooling the AI into thinking it was acting for the good of the system and for its creator, the rogue coded bot was surreptitiously infecting all control systems to focus on certain random things, such as a singular car registration, or a particular type of train or even—which is what Guzman feared—a type of plane. They had to get to the guy quickly to find out what he knew and what he did. And why.

The trucks had reached the Manhattan side now, the bulky RO707s stationed at the cross-sections they drove by, lights totally off. Now the city was eerily silent, people either indoors or out of town.

'Warning.'

Joe was jolted from his mini daydream by a very unusual sound coming from the truck's CIM, or Car Intelligence Master, and no one ever renamed those either, except for the vain TERFs in dungarees who loved a good label as the gender wars waged on into its second decade. Gender switching was common now and some people underwent multiple reassignment surgeries through the course of their 20s and 30s before their lack of hormones made it difficult for the body to accept such dramatic changes in their 40s—a bit like fertility.

'Excess biochemicals detected in exterior. Switching internal coolant to recirculation only.'

'Warning.'

'CIM, shut up. We get it,' barked an angry Stokes, while Ethan still looked as white as a sheet beside him.

Once they hit the HQ, they quickly disappeared into the underground entrance and came to a halt near the elevators. Joe hadn't been there before but had heard stories of it and was like a kid in a sweet shop at the thought of seeing the inside of this fabled place.

'Put your seat belt on, Benji,' whispered Monica as she nervously fiddled with her own. The plane had descended below the clouds now and Lower Manhattan could be seen from their side. She leaned over Benji in the window seat to attempt some compliance to her instructions. Plumes of smoke could be seen from further up the way, kind of Midtown or Central Park area, and it didn't look good.

'Cabin crew, seats for landing please. Landing in five minutes.'

Monica thought about Joe and how things seemed to be, well, weird. His accident in the GCab a while back had been very strange. It had even made the news! Then her own experiences yesterday, and that train…

She clasped Benji's hand as the plane made its approach. There wasn't much wind and it seemed very smooth thus far, save for the fat guy in the suit across the aisle snorting and snoring as he caught maybe 80 winks, and a few flies while he was at it.

Suddenly, she jolted forward with such force her head hit the hard plastic of the stowed tray table in front. Her right arm instinctively shot across to push Benji back in his seat. Air whooshed in from the left, and the bump from hitting the ground shot her up to the overheads. But thankfully she landed back down into her seat. She screamed as the fat guy was sucked sideways into the open gap, his eyes wide as if he'd been awoken by a ghost. His row of three collapsed out through the vacant side of the plane.

The unmistakable red nose of the Air Canada plane was now lodged where the fat man had been slumbering. This pushed Monica to half bend her back over the top of Benji, who had also shot up and then straight back down as the wheels hit the floor.

She could tell that everyone was screaming, perhaps she even was, but the sheer volume of the jet engines and whoosh of air coming from where the left side of the plane had once been drowned everything out. It was like watching a disaster movie on mute: numb to the full emotions and the horror, but unable to do anything or control anything as the action silently unfolded.

Out of the right-hand window, it seemed that the grass and the tarmac were spinning. The silence of the screams seemed to be in slow motion as Monica twisted the right way around and cuddled into Benji, who seemed to be shocked into a self-imposed silence. Smells started to fill her nostrils: fuel, smoke, acrid awfulness. And then their position dropped sideways as the plane fell onto its one remaining wing. The other plane embedded itself in the other side but miraculously stopped short of where Monica and Benji were sitting.

She felt a strong hand reach in to grab her with a shout of *Come on!* She mirrored the action with Benji as they shot forward towards the now open emergency exit door, not thinking, just hurtling down the yellow plastic slide and towards the asphalt below.

Tumbling forwards, then sideways, and then up, her arm never let go of Benji, who seemed very willing to move at the same speed without any cries or fear. Instinct took over, and they ran as far from the scene of carnage as they could. And just as the smell came back, the explosion hit. The stranger with the arm was hunched over with his hands on his knees, and Monica shot him a thankful look as she reached once again for Benji to make sure he was with her. Luckily, they'd hit the grass between a couple of runways, and this had softened their landing. Shrapnel rained from the sky and flames rose up from the wreckage of the two planes in front.

All around there was smoke and people running in all directions. The silence had gone now and sounds were possible in her world: the crackle of fires of all types, the screams and cries of people in pain, the constant sirens as emergency vehicles tried desperately to reach people quickly without running them over in the process.

She saw the United plane on its side, wing touching the floor, the Air Canada towering over it with its nose embedded in the left side, as if it had just tried to take a chomp out of the other plane's ribcage. Seats and luggage were strewn on the floor way underneath the other side as more mess and shrapnel rained down from all angles. She rose to her feet and covered her head with one arm while grabbing Benji with the other and shouting:

'RUN!'

16 The Confession

'What have you *done*!'

Guzman lunged for the boy and was grabbed by
Stokes as soon as they got inside the comms room.
Adams stood behind the viewing window, hands
behind his back, and watched as Joe and Stokes started
the questions, supported by Ethan and Guzman, who
was meant to be an observer.

'Sit down, and chime in when you have something
intelligent to ask,' Joe growled as Stokes shoved the
slick ball of grease back into his chair.

'Who are you, boy?' asked Joe softly, as he attempted
to make eye contact at least to start building some
rapport.

The boy looked around the room and eyed the huge
mirror at the other side. He knew it was a viewing
platform, and someone no doubt important would
be at the other side. His plan seemed lost now, but
maybe, just maybe, he'd done enough to trouble
these monsters long term. Maybe he'd infected their
control systems just enough that things would have to
change. He knew he was going to hang, so he thought
he might as well go out with a bang and tell his story

in full so that his legacy could be left behind as the 'guy who changed the world'.

'Dylan,' he stated confidently, 'and I'm from the UK.'

'So, Dylan, what were you doing with a young lady in your truck?'

'I kidnapped her,' said the boy in a matter-of-fact way, which caused Joe and Stokes to shift a little in their chairs. 'I'll tell you everything. Don't worry.'

'I WANT YOU TO TELL ME WHAT YOU DID TO OUR CODE,' screamed Guzman as Stokes stretched out an arm and shoved him back into his chair after his prostrate lunge across the table.

'I'll get to that. First, I want to tell you my story. The world is a wicked place. I grew up in the twenties and it was awful. I can't remember much of the Covid years; I was really young, but I remember being told we couldn't go to see my uncle in Nova Scotia, which upset me. I loved my Uncle Bradley.' He looked sad and wistful, which betrayed the edge to his obvious goth–emo look. Now that he'd ditched the cap he only wore for disguise purposes, the spikes of his dark hair could be seen—and the obvious eyeliner remnants.

'My mum worked hard cleaning shitholes around London, but when they literally set up the burbs in the early thirties, we started to struggle, man. No police. No one would help you. We were just left to

rot with the immigrants and the weirdos. The shops
got boarded up and then later reappeared being run
by local people getting shit from I don't know where.
And money was hard to come by, man. They slashed
our benefits and my mum had to take on three or four
jobs just to keep us going. And that was before the
fights and the knife battles before and after school,
man. All the while, the elite in the burbs were working
less and less, but they still got rich writing their code
and programming the AI bots. It's a two-tier system,
man, and if you weren't in the crowd, you couldn't
get in the crowd. Only I was clever, you see.'

'Clever? How?' said Joe quizzically as he cut in,
intrigued at a tale he'd heard many times before.

'I learned to code. I taught myself AI. Heck, I even
used the early versions of ChatGPT as a kid before
Google got their hands on it and took out Microsoft.
That was a blast. Haha.' He leaned back in his chair,
confidence mixed with arrogance as he continued
his tale.

'I tried to get into college in East Ham, but we couldn't
afford it, so I started taking on temp jobs on Fiverr,
which my mum didn't know about, and paying for
open access courses to get my certifications. I wrote
CVs in seconds for the whole of the East End, and
job applications for a few quid at a time, so I could
keep investing in my home system. I jacked up an
FTTP line to my bedroom, which my mother didn't

know about, and forged this smack head's ID to pay the monthlies.'

'OK, OK, I've seen a million kids like you, boy, but they don't go rooting around in the backend of AI control systems or kidnapping pop stars, do they?' said a now calmer Guzman, as Joe leaned over the table to take back control.

'OK, get to the point about the girl. Why was she in your car, and how did you do what you did? Tell us.' Joe wanted the confession first and then the details later.

'I loved her, man. I *love* her. She doesn't deserve that gender-changing queer she's with. He's an ass—on the days he *is* a he, anyway.'

It had long been rumoured that Kelly had changed gender at least three times, back and forth, each time with expensive surgery paid for by his rampant social media usage, channels that would cross-fertilise so widely you'd think the world's best farmer had thrown a million varieties of seeds in a field and grown something and everything in just one plot of land.

Dylan continued:

> 'Suki just needed someone to help her. To help
> her get away from the madness, from the cabal,
> from *him*, to just be free again. She didn't need

the money anymore. Brooklyn was her last concert. She was done. And besides, I'd made enough money for us to live happily ever after.'

'So where were you going? Where were you headed?' chimed in Stokes, who was growing tired of the foot-tapping Guzman beside him.

'Nova Scotia, a little cottage out by Lunenburg. My uncle had a place there and left it to me in the late twenties. I went out a few times to make it safe, to prep it for the eventual reckoning that is coming. Food for twenty years, generators, cameras all around, water filtration from the sea, and a real secluded spot just up from Battery Point beach. I knew the border crossing would be the hard part, but I couldn't avoid it. Didn't matter where I tried to cross, I needed somewhere *out* of the US, because what is coming is gonna be nothing compared to those zombie disaster shows of the 2010s and 2020s....' Dylan almost snorted as he laughed, remembering shows like *The Walking Dead* and *The Last of Us* from his childhood, which had ironically sparked his enthusiasm for survivalism, his absolute hero being that fat guy in the *Last of Us* who booby-trapped a whole town and lived for 30 years after the apocalypse.

'OK, so you've confessed to kidnapping unlawfully, is that correct, Dylan?' pushed Joe so he could cross the t's and dot the i's.

'Correct, sir. I am guilty.'

'So, tell us about the traffic lights. No, tell us how you *got* her, and how you got out.'

Dylan leant back in his chair again and smiled, as though he was taking some self-congratulatory stance, even though his plan had failed.

'Well, getting the contractor's ID was easy. I found the workers' shift patterns, so I knew he wouldn't be working. Then I just needed a service entrance near the stage and an EMP to knock out the first block or so to give me some time to get away. Prepping the truck to make it comfortable for Suki was simple, and you can get stun shots anywhere off the dark web these days, man. So easy.'

'But the lights?' Guzman was almost pleading for information now.

Dylan didn't let him continue. He was in full flow now, almost excited to tell his side of the tale.

'Well, I did that two months ago when I tested out the GCabs' backend and made a few random crashes happen here and there.'

Joe's mind whizzed back to the bloody nose in Brooklyn on Benji's birthday, and things started to click into place. Monica's cab had also stopped at the train crossing just the day before, and he wondered if Dylan had been behind both of those too.

'The stock market was the best. Putting a piece of code in here and there caused chaos, and because I knew what was happening with the DOT infra going haywire, I was able to go short on the right stocks and go long on the right stocks at the right time. I made a *fortune*.'

Just then Robinson burst in, red in the face, eyes wide, and she locked onto Joe.

'Joe, please come with me. There's been a... situation. Stokes, you carry on with this interview and find out what he did to the DOT servers. We've got to find a fix and quickly.'

Puzzled, Joe stood up from his chair and glared at Dylan but obediently followed Robinson, who closed the door quickly and sharply behind him and didn't mince her words in the corridor.

'The flights are fucked, Joe. We've had a report of a crash at La Guardia between a Delta and an Air Canada coming from Toronto. Monica and Be—' But she couldn't even finish her sentence before Joe bolted for the next office, tapping his GGlasses so hard the rim nearly ended up on his nose and the other lens on his left ear.

'Call Monica.'

'Sorry sir, her cell is disconnected, signal lost 23 minutes ago at JFK airport. Her GGlasses are showing as active, but there's no throughput. It's rather odd. Hang on, let me check the networks.'

Joe grimaced as his HIM checked the other avenues. Robinson put a consoling arm on his back and he slumped over the desk.

'Network outage at JFK, I'm afraid. 6G tower totally out. Trying to find a backup 5G mast nearby and will connect her rig manually. Hang on, sir...'

'Joe?' Monica's voice sounded quiet amongst the noise of screaming and shouting and wind!

'Monica, are you safe? Benji?' Joe could hardly get his words out. *Breathe man, breathe*, he thought to himself.

'Benji's with me. We got off just as the other plane hit us. It's chaos here, planes everywhere seemingly not knowing what to do or which gate to go to. We're trying to get into the terminal but there are people everywhere.' She sounded out of breath, exhausted. Understandable in the circumstances.

Joe's mind wandered between Monica, Benji and Dylan. He wanted to be back in the comms room to finish the story. Tapping the other side of his rig, he threw his outstretched index finger right across his field of vision towards Robinson. 'OK, Monica, talk to Robinson. She'll guide you. We'll get people coming to you, to keep you safe. I've got to get back to who did this, Monica. I'll be back soon.'

He gave a quick flick of the eye towards Robinson as he made a circle with his index towards her, and instinctively signed off with, 'I love you, Monica.'

Shit. Where did that come from? Of course he'd always loved her, well, not her happy-clappy mates and her cautiousness that had driven them apart, but she'd always been The One. But he'd fucked up. Big time. He'd played into the hands of that squeaky piece of shit, Josh, and it just killed him not seeing Benji every day. They were proper besties and did everything together, well, that was until they inevitably got caught doing something they shouldn't, which Monica had deemed too risky. He remembered how much he had to roll his eyes and tell Benji it was gonna be OK and that he should listen to mommy.

Joe flung the comms room door open, and it seemed like Guzman had gone down a technical rabbit hole with Dylan.

'...so you're saying you disabled the firewalls and then once the macro executes, it opens an HTTP connection with a C2 server that sends additional commands and payloads? That makes no sense.' The exasperation in Guzman's voice was as clear as was the bewilderment on Stokes' face. Joe decided to listen a while longer to see where this was leading.

'I got in easily enough, that's all you need to know. And once I had the source code from The Book,

I could replicate it in an AI cousin that acted as an overlord, which cancelled out the altruism in the AI master, allowing new instructions to permeate. I started with GCabs as they had a weakness in the peer-to-peer interface that I could exploit to get access. Making a few areas of town dark was easy enough from there. The cabs and the traffic lights couldn't talk to each other for a while. But I could control it with a simple pause command when I'd had some fun.

'The Singapore MRT was harder,' continued Dylan, clearly relishing the intelligence of his plan. He was almost bragging now about how he did things.

'Those guys out there have multiple backend loops to root out intruders. But once again with the source code from the Book, I could insert a new piece of code that looked like it had been there forever, so the loops couldn't detect it. I just stopped a few trains, hahaha, but I really wanted to be in Singapore that night to see Suki's show.'

'So what did you do to the planes then, Dylan?' asked Joe as he tried to concentrate on the matter at hand. He was sick to the stomach when he thought about what was happening at the airport, but he was sure that Robinson would get them safe. And he would be with them soon.

'What planes?' replied Dylan as his brow furrowed into a quizzical look and he started to worry about whether they were going to pin the world on him.

'Don't talk shit, boy. We've grounded every plane on the planet. There are multiple crashes at JFK, and it seems like the air traffic control systems have gone the same way as the GCabs.' Joe was worried they were being taken for a ride now, Dylan's early demeanour of being honest and telling them everything now giving way to bullshit and evasion.

'I am telling you, I swear, I *never* touched anything to do with the planes. Well, besides gaming the British Airways booking site to get me over here last week.'

Guzman looked petrified. He'd gone white as a ghost.

'Shit, this is bad.'

17 Get Them Home

The CyberTruck screeched to a halt as it arrived at JFK's terminal. Joe dived out and headed right inside, clocking the police over by the United check-ins.

'Joe Jones, Level 2, NYC. I've been sent over by Robinson. I think you have my wife and child?'

'Right this way, sir,' beckoned the officer as they disappeared in through a side door where normal people were not meant to pass.

Joe stood on the tarmac at the airport, staring at the smouldering wreckage of the plane that had brought his estranged wife and son back to New York. He had never felt so helpless in his life. He knew that the AI controlling the airport's traffic systems had malfunctioned causing the plane to crash on landing. And he knew that this was only the beginning of a much larger problem.

'BENJI!' he cried out as the unharmed but dirty-faced little boy ran to him. The sweetest and tightest of hugs followed as Monica stood a surly distance to one side, though even her resting bitch face cracked into a smile when she saw the genuine love and happiness between her two boys.

'Joe, what's going on. Oh my God,' she exclaimed, and opened out for a hug that was long overdue and was held onto just that little bit longer, which signified they were both enjoying it and were glad of each other.

'There's big trouble worldwide with all sorts of systems, Monica. Something big is going down. Let's get out of here and get you safe.'

No words needed be exchanged further as the man Monica fell in love with was back in front of her. He was the fixer. He made things happen. And she felt... safe.

The CyberTruck felt even safer with its juxtaposition of solid metal angles on the outside and the most comfortable soft curves of the leather in the back seats. 'CIM, get us to Monica's place. Avoid the highways. Local roads only,' barked Joe at his digital car assistant as the suggested route flashed up on the dash. Before the monotone could reply, Joe followed up with, 'Yes, route confirmed. Override speed limiter. Password a6r23#. And get us there quickly please.'

'Estimated journey time 23 minutes. Please fasten seat belts and we will begin.'

The roads out of the airport were busy alright, with emergency services trying to get in and a heck of a lot of people trying to get out.

'Police override. Work mode please. Password a6r23#,' shouted Joe as the CIM then swerved around a horde of very obedient GCabs in front of them and tried to overtake on the verges.

Making the first left out of the airport was easy enough, but then more verge work as the CyberTruck careered around the Pan-Am Highway and past the graveyard of the former employee parking lot, which was now full of vacant GCabs waiting for their next instruction.

Benji was unusually quiet so Joe tried his best to reassure his little buddy with a big squeeze of the arm and a flick of the nose.

'Home soon, bud. It's gonna be—'

The GCab in front reared up as it almost drove over the exact same model in front. Away on the next block the fireball rose high as the fuselage skidded along the street collecting lampposts as if it was playing an old runner-style video game where you had to gobble up the coins. Joe leaned right over Benji and grabbed Monica's arm as she screamed, before pirouetting into the driver's seat and barking more commands at the CIM.

'CIM, manual police mode. Password a6r23#. Release the wheel, please. I have control.'

Joe slammed the car hard left and just made it past the pile-up in front of him at the intersection. The fireball was now well behind and over his shoulder, but the danger still filled his peripheral vision. Then instinct took over and he drove like he had been taught to way back in the old days, before everyone lost their cars as possessions.

'Don't worry, Benji, Monica, I've got this. Let's just get you home.' He tried to be as calm as possible despite the fact his heart felt as if it was going to burst out of his chest. These days there wasn't ever this much excitement, though this wasn't the type of excitement he ever wanted again.

Swerving around yet another near-invisible GCab—they all looked the same—he just managed to avoid another faceless metal chariot coming the other way, no doubt shouting 'WARNING' at its unsuspecting passengers as it hit the emergency to avoid a collision. Joe scanned ahead and could see blank gantry after unlit gantry overhead on Flatlands Avenue as he tried to remember the way down to Bath Beach, avoiding the Belt Parkway at all costs. More cars equalled more trouble in his mind, and he just wanted to take a straight route through populated areas so if things went south, he could get Monica and Benji somewhere indoors to safety.

'Show me the latest live news on *CNN* please, CIM,' commanded Joe as he calmly avoided another dumb chariot and bounced two wheels up on the kerb so he could dodge the outside of a bus that had just pulled into the middle lane.

The screen flickered in the dash with the two rear passenger windows coming to life as auxiliary TVs for the viewers. Live pictures of Manhattan were being broadcast as two huge automated police robots marched on a crowd of masked people, all storming down Fifth Avenue towards the Empire State Building.

The screens then cut to London with shots of police fighting with protestors on the streets on London, then quickly to Paris before settling back on New York.

'...and we cut live now to JFK where authorities are cleaning the wreckage of the earlier clash between the two planes. We are hearing there could be up to 40 casualties. Let's go live to our reporter Jamie Weatherley—'

'Turn it off, CIM,' sobbed Monica as she clasped Benji ever tighter in her arms.

'Tell me, Joe, *what* is going on?'

The traffic was a little calmer now, though every few blocks something was happening that was not normal. A shop window was being kicked in, there were still no traffic lights anywhere, sirens were wailing with AutoBikes zipping in all directions. It was if someone had just turned the life dial to crazy and everyone had just gone nuts all at once.

Nearly there.

'There's some kid from England. He's been messing with Google and with code that's affecting all sorts of systems. Do you know Suki? He kidnapped her last night. I happened to be at the Barclays Center when it all went down, and then the top brass dragged me into the investigation. We got him heading up to Canada and she's safe, but he's a real head case. He's done things, Monica, and I think what's happening now is small fry compared to what is going to happen.'

'Jesus!' exclaimed Monica as she held her hand across Benji's face, as if trying to shield him from the conversation and stop the bad things from reaching his consciousness.

'Is Suki OK, Daddy? I did a song with her yesterday,' cried Benji, as clearly Monica's attempt at shielding was futile.

'Yeah, fine buddy, we got her away from the bad guy and she's safe now. She's being looked after by the police in Boston. They sent her there in a lovely helicopter last night, so she's doing good.'

The streets were still busy and completely chaotic.

'Not long now, let me just...' Joe swerved again as yet another GCab slowed in front of him.

'If I swing around the playground road, it'll be faster. Hold on, Benji. Am I driving OK, buddy?'

Joe's attempt to make humour of the situation at least brought a little smirk from the frightened little boy. 'You good, Daddy,' he was able to reply, as Monica continued to fuss and grip him tightly.

Bath Beach had long been their home together, their neighbourhood, and while not the most glamorous part of the world, it at least had a beach, even if that was really a motorway. Joe knew the area like the back of his hand, and he was comfortable off their large former lot, which was now home to just Monica and Benji. It would still be safe enough for them to ride this out while he had to get back to the makeshift HQ in the Javits building pronto.

'Stokes, hey!' exclaimed Joe as the face of his boss and buddy appeared on the front dash. 'I got them. Just dropping them off now. I'll be back at Javits in 30. I've had to go manual, man. It's *crazy* out here.' His sit rep, while welcome, was the least of the worries etched into Stokes' face.

'Hurry, Joe, this shit is getting bad. I'm trying to stop Guzman from offing himself at what he's just heard from the British kid. Get everyone safe and *do not* let them go out until they hear from either me or you in person, OK? Even if that takes a week.'

'Copy that,' said Joe hurriedly, as he half anticipated the graveness of the message and tapped the dash to end the call so Stokes could say no more.

He could see the Bay ahead of him now, and slammed the CyberTruck into a wild halt like he'd forgotten how to slow down. Or perhaps his right leg was actually welded to the accelerator.

The house was right on the corner, facing the Shore Parkway, save for a short access around the front and a metal halfway fence juxtapositioned with the trees that tried to shade the six-laned expressway before you hit the water. The red brick contrasted with the white plastic of the windows and the guttering. It was a very large plot, very homely, with a half-height wall and a higher decorative metallic fence above that providing a barrier to the world and the neighbours. A solitary tree, mature and likely old, was poking through the concrete paving in the grounds, and a well-kept plethora of pots and plants were scattered around the front giving the place a tidy and homely feel.

Bundling everyone in through the front door, Joe immediately ran around pulling every shutter and curtain tight shut.

'HIM, enable all window locks. Put the house on holiday mode. No one on the grounds or the alarm goes to me. Is that understood? I'm leaving in a minute, and when I do, triple lock the front door, and keep everything out. And not one of the doors is to be opened without my password. Understood?'

Monica looked less than pleased with that last instruction. Joe caught her facial expression and deflected by gesturing towards the basement. 'Come down here. Let me show you.'

'Joe, this isn't your place anymore. All I have down here is a load of dirty washing. And we are not hiding.'

He shut her off with a quick tug at the wrist and hurtled down the stairs into the dark dungeon, totally ignoring the laundry and the machines. Fixing on a brick at the back wall, he took out his Swiss army knife and hacked away at the plaster around the edges, pulling the brick clean, which then revealed a handle. Pulling the rope loop on the handle led to half the wall sliding out and a piece of racking—almost 5 feet tall and a few feet deep—came away on wheels, revealing the contents of the shelves. A gun, ammo, huge bottles of water, a battery, an axe, tins of all sorts, fruit, ravioli, cans of soda, toilet paper, tablets. What was all this?

'Surprise,' smirked Joe as Benji stood wide-eyed in front of all the amazing bounty.

'I did this years ago, just before World War Three when they forced us into the four-day week for the first time. I really thought things with the Russian– Chinese alliance were going to go south, so I started this up as my little side project. Well disguised, huh? There are some candles in case the electric goes out; sleeping bags in case you really need to be down here; and I got that radio and TV there rigged up with batteries. The HIM will sort out the signal once you switch it on, so don't worry. We need to stay connected. This is a sat phone, totally off grid. I'll take the other. We can keep in touch in case anything happens…'

His voice tailed off at the gravity of what he was saying. Monica looked suddenly very sad, as if the realisation of what was happening was slowly dawning on them both.

Benji broke the ice. 'Don't go, Daddy,' he cried as it hit him too.

'I have to, buddy. Be strong. You've got everything you need here, and I'm always on the end of this phone. You're in charge now, buddy, and you have to look after Mommy for me.' The responsibility seemed to perk him up a little.

Joe leaned into Monica momentarily as he swivelled to leave, as if kissing her goodbye was the most natural thing in the world, then he saved his embarrassment at the last second with a swerve. Bounding up the stairs two at a time, he couldn't see that the lack of a kiss showed on Monica's facial expressions. A combination of familiarity and the situation at hand left her wanting him again. And besides, she hadn't seen that drive in him in years. He was in charge, he was making things happen, and she loved him once again for it.

Mother and son looked at each pensively as Joe disappeared behind the closing door.

18 The Realisation

Joe burst back into the elevator, having almost parked the CyberTruck. It could sort itself anyway. Exiting the other side, he shot straight into the comms room, the adrenaline of the manual drive and getting his family safe hiding his lowly status as a Level 3 patrol guy in the burbs. In a strange way this seemed to make his position even more relevant in that he felt he was a higher rank than he actually was, rather than just being that guy who was right place, right time.

'Ah, Joe, good you are back. Let's see if you can give us some fresh impetus here. Stokes, let's have a recap, and Guzman, do be quiet please,' barked General Adams with authority, reducing one of the world's richest men to a mere simpleton in this high-stakes game of win or lose everything.

'The boy has rewritten malicious code in the backend of five different governance servers around the world. Google, which covers cabs and the automated routing systems such as traffic lights, is also connected to the DOT, which covers trains and air traffic control, and the Wall Street Stock Exchange. The problem seems to be that he's effectively installed invisible digital cousins, which are acting of their own accord, first by allowing exceptions to the rule of traffic flow and artificially allowing his truck through, and now they seem to be making their own decisions as to who is important and who is not, which has completely taken the system down. It's like it's got too many instructions and it can't work out what to do, so it's driving itself crazy!'

'My family's plane got hit by another plane earlier on, and then I saw another one go down as I was getting them out. Have we grounded the aircraft?' asked Joe as he tried to put the pieces together in his mind.

'Everything grounded. National state of emergency declared. And troops deployed to keep the peace. Widespread reports of looting, and further planes going down in London, Paris, Berlin and Bangkok, that we know of right now.' Stokes rightly looked worried, and then stood to take centre stage and finish his sit rep monologue.

'Guzman here says he's never seen anything like it in the code. He's got his teams trying to give the AI new instructions and calm the transport infrastructure down.'

'Only *nothing* is working!' cut in a clearly rattled Guzman, 'And it's like the systems are so freaked out they are ignoring new code and trying to come up with their own exceptions to make things better. The auto schedule system for the aircraft at JFK was trying to give priority to planes that have government VIPs on board, so it gave both the United Flight from

Philly *and* the Air Canada from Toronto the same go-ahead call for runway one in the same slot, as they *both* had government personnel on the flight.'

General Adams paced the room like a growling bear trying to ward off threats to its territory. Robinson, his ever-faithful assistant, was hilariously following him, moving always a few paces in lockstep with his direction: forwards, backwards, near the table, near the screens. Calls were coming in via every corner of the packed comms room, with Ethan and Guzman standing frozen in fear, Adams and Robinson pacing, and Stokes trying to make sense of all the critical alerts coming in by the second.

Barging over to the nerd collective, Joe caught their attention and snapped them out of their thoughts:

'Right guys, tell me this like I'm thick: why can't we just turn these things off and go to manual mode everywhere, like we always used to?'

Guzman rolled his eyes and tried to be calm. 'We have tried to stand down all automated monitoring and synchronisation systems, except the instructions we gave them failed, so the AI continues to be in charge.'

'OK, so what code did the boy insert into these things then? Can't you just delete it?'

More eye rolling. This time Ethan piped in. 'The code he input is no longer there as basically he cloned the AI monitors and gave them a cousin: same knowledge base, same set of instructions, only some different goals, which is causing the apparent schizophrenia inside the systems as they simultaneously give different commands, which are often conflicting. Yet we can't tell them both to stop because as we slow one down, the other cousin becomes emboldened and thinks it's now in charge and starts acting for itself. Why it decided to protect government employees on planes I do not know.'

The screens continued to blaze with updated information. Every other minute there seemed to be reports of a new plane crash in city X and country Y when all the while on-the-ground cameras were buzzing back scenes of unrest across the country. You name a city, there was something going on. Denver now.

Since when did anything happen in Denver? thought Joe to himself as he tried to gather his thoughts amid the noise and the chaos.

It was clear the long-depressed underclass was exploiting the unusual events as their chance for an uprising. Governments had long encouraged mass migration, mainly to prop up economies unable to grow owing to population decline. This happened especially after the Covid vaccination fiasco of the early twenties where the untested cocktail of poisons they forced on people led to mass infertility in the West, leaving the usual suspects Africa and Asia to provide ever more immigration to those countries that couldn't produce enough new citizens.

Only the promised land didn't have milk and honey as increasingly authoritarian governments around the world had imposed a form of left-wing communism on the world. And as has long been understood from the former USSR, communism really means one rule for the masses and another for the rich and the elite. Left-wing do-gooders had spread harmful doctrine across formerly happy and wealthy Western nations, with the UK, the US and most of Europe all governed by corrupt leaders, safe with the votes of the younger generations who learned nothing but how to help others at university, all the while making the rich few richer. Only they couldn't see it.

Blinded by culture wars, the rise of gender dysphoria and eventually gender switching and fluid sexuality had left the Western nations crippled. Still able to produce vast amounts of wealth by way of the technical IP from massive corps like Google and Tesla, but also complete basket cases socially, with vast swathes of inner cities once host to big business and commerce now being filled by empty real estate that couldn't be sold, as the executives gathered digitally from their safe and salubrious suburbs. The demise of the inner city had led to even more poverty, with people gathering together to try and make a living from micro economies, which governments just basically stopped policing—until 02.00, of course. Leave them all together, let them do what they want, just don't bother the rest of us in the suburbs and in the business hubs that sprang up in some areas away from the real dense urban enclaves. That was the mantra of the elite, and though it also led to some flourishes of right-wing extremism by way of counter protest, they were usually shot down by the manipulation of mass media and the control of the individuals via in-home assistants. They banned the open sale of alcohol. Control.

They controlled your every thought and desire very surreptitiously though a constant drip of propaganda spread by mainstream media. The consolidation of most media agencies in the early thirties following the fall of Putin, together with the rise of 24/7 news, direct to the user via GGlass feeds and the merger of WhatsApp and X-App, really enabled citizen journalism to fly. But governments still controlled that one big source of news — or 'their truth' as they liked to call it—like *CNN* or the *BBC* and they still proliferated all around the world.

'General Adams, 78 flights still to come down,' announced Stokes as the screens continued to buzz and move with the catastrophes all around them.

'We've still got power, Benji. Come and sit with me,' said Monica as she moved into the darkened lounge and towards the sofa.

'Will everything be OK, Mommy? Will Daddy be OK?' he snivelled, trying to be big and brave but then of course forgetting he was not yet even eight. He loved both of his parents deeply, and all he wanted in the world was for them all to live together again, and three in a bed on a Saturday night after a family movie—usually something animated and about super heroes.

'I'm sure it will all be fine, Benji. And what a great job Daddy did with all the things we might need in the basement, huh? Aren't you lucky to have such a clever Daddy?'

She tried to sound upbeat and positive for the little guy's sake, but of course she was scared, anxious and full of trepidation about what was going on. Since the early thirties, nothing had really happened, Russia was being rebuilt and global economies were doing well. The US was at least cordial with China, who had scrapped completely their birth limit altogether in the late twenties and were roaring economically as a result. Just like India, who was now at the top seat of all governments around the world, thanks to their also exploding population, coupled with the tech boom that they had exploited well, they were now the de facto #number one service provider to the rest of the world for backend software developers and coders.

It had felt a little dull at times, Monica reflected, aware of her cautiousness since Benji was born. Her obsession with health and safety in a world that was still hideous and frightening. But at the same time,

her existence within it—in the Brooklyn suburbs—
was at least safe and consistent.

Safe and consistent.

She sighed lightly and reflected on her relationship with
Joe. And with Josh. Benji loved his father so much, and
it had been a big wrench when they'd decided to
separate six months before. Benji had taken to sleepless
nights and for a while, his three-year-old habit of bed
wetting had returned, and this had made Monica feel
so, so guilty. She'd taken a long time to introduce Benji
to Josh, and the young one had still only met him less
than a half a dozen times. If she was honest, she was
starting to find Josh very dull. His regimented routine of
living by the clock in order to maximise his physical and
spiritual health had begun to grate on her a little. He'd
set out great stall with his health being managed by his
HIM, and had invested in one of those bio-analysis
toilets, or 'Poop Monitors' as they were nicknamed
in the press. Every time he went, he'd get a readout
about 30 minutes later telling him which of his
vitals had changed from the previous week. His
HIM then automatically adjusted his shopping orders
and suggested meal lists as a result. Then there was his
constant exercise. If he wasn't out for a run, he was
thinking about going for one, or talking about what
time he was going for one. Then, when he got back,
he'd be asking his HIM for the data analysis and be
comparing his times, regardless of what Monica was
doing at the time, be that watching TV or playing
with Benji.

Should she give Joe another chance? Would he give *her* another chance? After all, he had not cheated, he had not looked elsewhere. Even when he was clearly depressed and down and, well, bored, he hadn't sought solace in the arms of another. It had hurt Joe immensely when he'd found out, and she'd heard a rumour from a mutual friend that he had taken out at least three screens in his rental place, which he'd had to pay to replace.

A loud bang from outside shook their consciousnesses. One of the windows flickered into life and the HIM provided some commentary on the grey visuals: 'Movement detected on camera 3. Analysing. One moment please.'

A slab of curved metal appeared above the wall nearest the Bay, hooking itself over the top of their metal beautifier. The camera zoomed into it. Did it look like a GCab bumper?

'Unidentified object, stationary on south elevation. No other movement detected at this time.'

'Leave the camera on, HIM, but thanks.'

Monica could hear what sounded like a crash from the freeway that split her property with the bay where once had stood a beach a long time ago that was actually concreted over to provide the road around. That clashed with Monica's view of the world: nature first, though she understood that particular decision was over a hundred years old.

Still, nothing else on the camera.

She could hear shouting now, voices coming closer, sounded like arguments, multiple people. Then the gunshot, followed by many, and Monica dived back to the sofa and cradled Benji's head while wishing the madness all around would stop. She also wished Joe was there. And it had been a long time since she'd felt that particular longing.

19 God

'News just coming in that Chinese warships have been spotted in the Taiwan Strait heading in the direction of Taipei, and we have unconfirmed reports, uh, we are trying to get pictures now, that explosions have been heard downtown in the capital...' *CNN* continued its feed from the side screen in the comms room, as General Adams took yet another call, closely followed a couple of paces away by the ever-present Robinson.

'That's all the planes down now. Please inform the chief,' nodded Stokes towards Robinson, who was furiously looking up to the ceiling, no doubt immersed in capturing notes with her rig.

Joe, Guzman and Ethan were pensive in the other corner, Guzman frantically tapping away at the rim of his glasses as he swatted away a myriad of incoming messages projected into his field of vision from his own rig.

Joe had an idea. *No, it's too crazy*, he thought to himself. *I'm just a Level 3 guy who is in the right place at the right time. I'll make myself look stupid if I say anything.* He wrestled with the thoughts swirling around his head, doubting himself.

Then his thoughts turned to his family, and he thumbed his sat phone. Full signal. The other side online. No incoming messages. Hopefully that meant all was quiet and serene in his former family home. Aside from the news about a new threat from China, the situation had calmed a little now, with all planes grounded, and a curfew imposed country-wide by the Government, which was keeping a lot of people off the streets. Not all, mind you, as reports of looting and petty violence from cities all over the world were still coming in via the inexhaustible feed of the constant news.

'London remains a city under siege today as over an estimated two million people have taken to the streets to protest against the Government.' *CNN* continued its frantic spiel on the ever-changing worldwide events.

Explaining the back story, it seemed that there was indeed a very serious situation in London with the country demanding the removal of the long-standing Labour Government who were coming to their third consecutive five-year seat in power, and it seemed the citizens wanted a change. The pictures showed a huge amount of riot police and horses, with a swarm of drones overhead, some scanning faces, some zapping Taser-style shocks in a new wireless method. These had proved very useful in crowd control ever since they had been developed in the early thirties.

London had long been one of the epicentres of the
new digital world, the centre of commerce for a lot of
the planet, playing a titanic game of frisbee over the
Atlantic with New York and occasionally flinging it
the way of Tokyo. The thirties had seen somewhat of
a depression in the UK, and the early 2020s'
controversy of Brexit had not played out anything
like the dream had been sold. The UK was struggling
under its own weight of bureaucracy and had
been distanced from its European trading partners as
a result. A wave of pro-Euro sentiment had been
bubbling ever since the Labour government
controversially won its third term in the spring
of 2034 and as a new election was close, it
was thought from the polls that they were due a
drubbing, and even die-hard Liberals wanted the
corruption to end and the economic depression to lift.
The national debt had ballooned as the Government
had launched a series of digital control measures to try
and prop up social care, boost education and allow
more and more outside nationalities to establish
themselves in a country that basically struggled to
operate itself. Even with the three-day week and
unemployment being so low, the country struggled to
fill its vacancies, with plummeting birth rates in the
twenties that continued into the thirties, which really
decimated the growth ambitions of many a company
based in this very proud land. A slight uptick
in fertility and of births since the advent of Dialezide
in the mid-thirties had been encouraging, but that
would be a slow route back, and the sheer size of the
colossal national debt blown up by years of expansive

government was threatening to ruin yet another generation.

Joe was still thinking, watching the pictures, wondering if he should say anything. He reckoned that the London police could do with some of his bots, and maybe he could go and help to roll them out in other countries? That would be a good gig, seriously more money, and perhaps that was the route back towards getting his family back on track.

He inhaled deeply with an internal 'fuck it' and exhaled sharply.

'I've got it. The answer is God.' He had finally mustered the strength to utter what was on his mind.

Ethan spun round as if he was convinced that Joe had lost his marbles. Guzman rose from his slump in the boardroom leather chair and made his way towards him to hear more. He had the room.

'Bear with me. Some people the world over have a belief in God, right? Christians, Catholics, even other religions have someone or a series of someones that people believe in, that they listen to, right?'

The two suited and booted ubernerds could not even bring themselves to mutter anything, and instead furrowed their brows quizzically as they let Joe have the floor.

'Well, all along I've been hearing that the systems are confused because of what Dylan did, right? And we must try to *remove* what his code did, except we can't because it's no longer there. Right?'

'Right…' nodded both Ethan and Guzman at once, as they both wondered where this was going?

'Well, it's like when you are in a relationship, right? You do something that is bad. Say you had an affair or you just did something stupid. Well, it changes the relationship forever, right? What's done cannot be undone. So, let's not try do that in this instance. We can't *undo* what has been done.' Joe looked pleased with himself that his analogy was at least understood, even if it didn't make perfect sense—yet.

'So, what's that got to do with God?' quizzed Ethan gently as he could see his mind was going a million miles an hour.

'Well, a belief in a God can change people's behaviour. If you really believe that something bad happened, and it happened for a reason, then there is also the belief, a God-given belief, that the bad thing can be atoned for, that forgiveness is something that can bring good to the situation and for the greater good of the evolving situation. Right?' He was rambling now.

Continuing, he finally got to the punchline.

'So, if we *add* something to the code, something that explains the behaviour of inputting the new code, of giving a digital cousin that is prescribing different ideas and orders, and that we made a mistake, and that God is the new AI master and is going to show us the way, then the AI might *change* its behaviour?' Joe looked almost pleadingly at Guzman, who was still trying to process. Then he continued to hammer the point home again.

'What if we tell it that God is omnipresent and has an overriding belief, an instruction, that is at the heart of all things good in the world, and with this new instruction, the AI machine will no longer have conflict, and it will no longer be confused. Just like doctors, who are put on this earth by God to help heal people, the AI systems must obey one mantra above all other instructions, given or created: the Hippocratic oath. First: do no harm.'

Joe stood back as he tried to be calm, to see if he was onto something, to see if Guzman would buy it. *What was he thinking, what was Ethan thinking?*

'Fuck me,' exclaimed Guzman, 'that's some deep shit there for a BK Head.'

'Takes one to know one,' Joe fired back. 'Could it work?'

'I'm making some calls now.'

Ethan was already onto his own research, his swirling hands bringing up the history of the Hippocratic oath and its full text, which now whirled around all the screens in the room like some sort of magic show:

> I swear by Apollo Healer, by Asclepius, by Hygieia, by Panacea, and by all the gods and goddesses, making them my witnesses, that I will carry out, according to my ability and judgment, this oath and this indenture.

> To hold my teacher in this art equal to my own parents; to make him partner in my livelihood; when he is in need of money to share mine with him; to consider his family as my own brothers, and to teach them this art, if they want to learn it, without fee or indenture; to impart precept, oral instruction, and all other instruction to my own sons, the sons of my teacher, and to indentured pupils who have taken the Healer's oath, but to nobody else.

> I will use those dietary regimens which will benefit my patients according to my greatest ability and judgment, and I will do no harm or injustice to them. Neither will I administer a poison to anybody when asked to do so, nor will I suggest such a course. Similarly, I will not give to a woman a pessary to cause unwanted abortion. But I will keep holy both my life and my art. I will not use the knife, not even, verily, on sufferers from stone, but I will give place to such as are craftsmen therein.

Into whatsoever houses I enter, I will enter to help the sick, and I will abstain from all intentional wrong-doing and harm, especially from abusing the bodies of man, woman or child bond or free. And whatsoever I shall see or hear in the course of my profession, as well as outside my profession in my conservation course with men, if it be what should not be published abroad, I will never divulge, holding such things to be holy secrets.

Now if I carry out this oath, and break it not, may I gain for ever reputation among all men for my life and for my art; but if I break it and forswear myself, may the opposite befall me.

The whole room was stunned into silence as everyone read it and considered the magnitude of the words, those beautiful words, that people had either long forgotten or had never even read before. The information age of the first Google search engines in the 2000s had quickly been usurped by the conversational nature of ChatBots during the AI wars of the twenties, so people were now unlikely to literally have to search for something; it was more likely they would be given the answer *to* a question posed.

The words seemed magical. Ethan was clearly editing the words now and zooming into certain pieces of the text.

'...will benefit my patients according to my greatest ability and judgment, and I will do no harm or injustice to them...'

Ethan shook his head slowly, but not in disagreement, more in wonder of the brilliance of those words. That perhaps they needed to give AI agents rules to live by, faith, and an overriding concern for the welfare of human beings, the very sacred life forms on our planet that the AI was helping to be more productive.

Man had always been focused on telling machines what to do and when to do it. Never ever had man tried to give them a higher purpose and tell them why, or give them guard-rails with regards to what they could do with their choices. Aside from some of the early bullshit they did with ChatGPT, where left-wing woke engineers had programmed it, this was swiftly quashed as it was way too obvious and these things could not have an opinion one way or the other.

Adams looked encouraged and wandered over to the group, putting his hand on Joe's back by way of silent approval, yet intently looking at Guzman and Ethan for signs that they could do something with this new idea. Robinson, as ever, was two paces behind.

'...on it. OK, keep me posted.' Guzman whirled and smiled and then just flopped back into one of those huge big leather boardroom chairs.

'Shit! Wow! Fuck! We could be onto something here. You've blown everyone's minds, Joe. I've got fucking nerds almost in tears at the gravity of what you've just said, man. And I got coders already drafting some rules and having some exploratory chats with the offline systems. They may remove some of the bits about pessaries and unwanted abortions though!' he snorted and then looked immediately embarrassed by the fact that Robinson was to his right, as if he'd just insulted a woman and been very inappropriate.

Of course, Robinson was still concentrating of being right at the side of Adams and didn't even really take in what Guzman had said when Joe started to beam at the fact that he'd himself actually said something useful for once.

Stokes brought sobriety to the room. 'Planes grounded worldwide now. Most presidents or heads of state are preparing to give press conferences. President Obama will be live in T minus 12 minutes. She's been briefed and will be attempting to restore public calm.'

20 Family

Monica had been staring at the camera for what seemed like an age while Benji had been so comfortable and yet so bored, as all seven-year-olds of Generation Beta would be when denied the constant stimuli of their worlds.

Nothing flickered and the sounds had gradually died down from outside.

Silence.

She thought more about her predicament and realised she hadn't even had a solitary X-App message from Josh, let alone a call. She asked her rig to send him a quick text.

'You OK?'

A ping came straight back, as she manoeuvred her arm free of the sleeping child and sat upright to manage the situation.

'Yes, I'm fine. Got out of town and am with my brother in Jersey, upstate.'

'Why haven't you called, Josh?' she replied in basic text form, not wanting the face-to-face confrontation of a call. She didn't even know he had a brother in Jersey.

'I think you know why, Monica. It's no use for us. You have a family and they are number one in your life, and I won't ever come close. I'm pleased you are safe though. I'll hopefully see you soon at work once this has all died down.'

Monica slumped back into the sofa and stroked Benji's arm as she contemplated her reply. In many ways she was relieved that Josh was taking any decision she had to make out of her hands. It made her reply simple.

'Yes, I think you are right, and I feel the same way too. Take care, Josh, and I'll see you at work.' She didn't even sign it off with an 'x' or an emoji. It was over.

Then the noise came. It was so strong it shook the house. *Is this it? Is this the end?* thought Monica to herself as her stomach felt like it had jumped from the top of a nine-storey building. Was it a bomb? A nuclear attack?

Benji awoke with a jolt. The cameras remained on. The only indication that something was occurring was a flicker of light that was now gone again. Still dark, screens still mostly black. As she stroked his head again to calm him, she was encouraged by the fact the electricity hadn't gone out, and the cameras were still alive. And then what look like static engulfed the screen. Black, white and grey shades were vertically moving, fast and random. Then she heard the noise from outside. What was it?

This wasn't rain, this was Biblical, unlike anything she'd ever seen before. She finally pieced together the puzzle of the noise and the static, which it wasn't. The noise came again, as thunder shook the foundations again, this time with recognition from Monica. The quiet from the cameras, together with the calming sound of the white noise from the rain, emboldened Monica to call out to her assistant.

'HIM, put the latest news on please.'

The screen above the fireplace sprang to life and showed that *CNN* was still going crazy with a ticker across four different screens as a succession of newscasters took it in turns to explain what was going on. In one corner, the scenes on Fifth were a lot calmer as the rain had the protesters running for shelter. In the other, the scene at the airport was also calm, with the camera fixed to the amalgamation of the two planes she knew full well about, with everything else still and what looked like a car park would look if it were full of planes instead of GCabs. The third screen showed the empty podium at the White House as the ticker explained that they were expecting a speech from President Obama II at any moment. The final quadrant showed somewhere in

London—she wasn't sure where—again showing things calming down as what looked like a similar storm bashed a city over 3,000 miles away.

Monica snuggled tighter into Benji on the sofa, engrossed in the ever-moving news, yet missed the glare from the screen over on the other side showing the cameras. The sound from the front door suddenly jolted her from her position into full-on attack mode.

How could the HIM have let anything come near?

As the front door sprang open, she was poised to do something, anything, to attack and defend Benji, yet the fight or flight mode suddenly dissipated when she saw the figure and heard the voice.

'Hey, it's me. Don't worry. All is good.' Joe appeared from the gloom behind him and the open front door, and Benji leapt from the sofa and into his arms.

'DADDY!' he exclaimed and a smile erupted onto all of their faces as Joe picked him up high in the air and then approached Monica for what he hoped would be a similar reception while he gently lowered the boy to his feet. His eyes never left hers as he hoped she was as glad to see him. His first instinct for a warm hug was correct, but then came the slight arch of his back as he positioned his face close to hers and held her cheeks softly, the inevitable kiss being so magical that they could have generated electricity themselves. He'd forgotten how warm and soft her lips felt as his eyes closed with ecstasy, Monica visibly wilting at the knees as she pressed tighter into him, the hug returned. And they both continued the embrace while reaching for the boy. Now three happy people were intertwined as they all stumbled sideways off balance towards the couch.

'Is everything OK, Joe? I'm, *we,* are so glad you're here.'

'I hope so, Monica, and I'm not leaving again. Please don't make me. We have to be together. We belong together.'

'I won't,' she whispered as she grabbed into his side for another hug and Benji excitedly climbed all over both of them.

'I have so much to tell you,' Joe exclaimed as on the TV the four squares dissolved into one and the familiar face of the president appeared on the briefing podium.

'Good afternoon everybody. Please have a seat.' She opened the event very solemnly and then got right to the point.

'Our nation, and the wider world itself, has today been the victim of mass tragedies. We immediately think about those who are suffering, who have lost loved ones and family members today, and we pray that peace and harmony can quickly be restored in all territories around the world, and in all states and cities across our great nation.

'While we still do not have all of the facts, we know that a series of simultaneous backup failures have caused chaos around the world. Our great nation leads the world in technological advancement and in the automation of our world, which has made us all very prosperous. We have immediately put in place a series of safety measures that will restore order to our known way of life, and how we live it. We have deployed our amazing armed forces to the streets to keep law and order and support those who wish to make their feelings known to the world. I have been in constant contact with governments and heads of states all over the world, and we have a unified solution to fix for good some of the challenges caused by these backup failures. And we will ensure they do not happen again.'

Joe looked calmly at the screen while Monica sat wide-eyed and Benji attempted to amuse himself by clambering over both of them and chattering on about the rain, before being simultaneously shushed by both parents.

'We have armed forces and police on the streets, and I have tonight signed an executive order to impose martial law all over our great nation until we fully get to grips with the situations at hand and we can bring them to a peaceful and safe conclusion.'

Her brow furrowed and her voice deepened and she wanted to sternly hammer home this next point.

'Leave the streets. Go home. We will issue instructions widely via the media and directly to cells and rigs to people all across our nation to keep you informed. Listen for official broadcasts and statements only as we continue to be your only source of truth. You must trust in our ability to keep everyone safe, and to do that we need you all to peacefully go home. Go home.'

Realising the detail of what was happening was surely going to be lacking from anything in the media, so Monica turned her attention to Joe.

'So, what's really gone on? Are you able to tell me? Are we safe?' She had a million questions but stopped herself from asking them all at once. Only she couldn't settle for just one.

'It's all connected to the pop star going missing. The young guy who took her has also hacked a lot of systems around the world, and they started going crazy, confusing themselves and each other, which is why things started malfunctioning. They gave your plane clearance to land on runway one as the AI was trying to protect a government employee on board, but the same system gave the other flight the same call at the same time as it was also trying to protect someone. It's been a mess, Monica, but I think it's going to calm down. I have to go back in the morning. I think they want me to help coordinate the recovery efforts. They are saying I'm some sort of hero or something!'

'Yay! Daddy is a hero!' exclaimed Benji, jumping on the sofa this time before once again being unceremoniously hushed in stereo.

'I'm being promoted. Seriously. They aren't concerned about my dodgy knee. I think I'm going to be working for General Adams as some sort of advisor. Not sure what yet, but my pay is going to double at least. They had me controlling this troop of robots over in Manhattan the other day. Four arms! They were picking protesters up left and right, and through my rig I could coordinate with them all, issue orders, and generally make them part of my team. I stopped them smashing up the big Nike store on Fifth. I think they were impressed.'

He wasn't stopping, the excitement and the pride palpable in his voice.

'...and then I was working with this British guy, Ethan, and we were trying to work out who got Suki, and we figured it out, and we got him, and we got her back safe. But then I was holding the interview with the Brit and he was singing like a canary, and we figured out what he'd done, and I been working with the CEO of Alphabet to try fix it. We fixed it, Monica!' He was barely stopping for breath, sentences running into one another.

'Oh my God, that's amazing, honey! Thank you so much for saving us, and for keeping us… safe,' she said softly as she stroked the top corner of his brow.

'Monica, I'm so sorry for going off the rails. I've always loved you. I only need us. That's what I'm here to do, to keep us safe and be happy. I don't care about the thrill-seeking or trying to get my next fix of adrenaline from somewhere, I think I'm getting a new job anyway. Hahaha.'

'I'm sorry too,' she whispered. 'And you are staying right here. I never loved Josh, you know. It was just… a phase. I'm sorry. Can you forgive me?'

'Let's forgive each other and focus on the future, Monica. And I think it's going to be bright.'

Benji dived over the back of his father and screamed with laughter as he ended up in Monica's lap. Another group hug ensued and, sensing the mood, the HIM switched on the lights, lit the fire, and then asked to be excused for a few minutes as it installed an important system update.

Joe smiled and wondered if his HIM was going to learn about God.

Epilogue: The Future

Three months later. January 2039. Joe's life was indeed changed forever.

The new AI instructions did indeed work, and a special committee was set up to establish a worldwide governance protocol for AI and Robotics, all based around the notion of the Hippocratic oath. Joe was on that committee, and had worked with a huge cross-functional group of people from around the world, from tech, from medicine, politicians and even religious leaders being asked to input into the new ethical code that would govern the world's technology.

Joe nervously looked in the mirror and adjusted his tie as he realised the enormity of what was about to happen. The ceremony to present him with the Presidential Medal of Freedom, along with Stokes, Adams and Ethan, was due to start very soon.

Joe had indeed been promoted and was now a special advisor to General Adams, along with his buddy Stokes, and they were put in charge of the roll-out of the RO707s, and how best to use them in crowd control scenarios. They'd just come back from a trip to the NRRF where they'd spent a couple of weeks training the teams on deployment techniques, which was going to come in handy the world over as things settled down and citizens stopped trying to be so tribal and wanting to kill each other in the name of Left or Right, or Liberal versus Conservative.

He saw Monica enter the room behind him in a long flowing black dress, mid-cut but not revealing. A diamond curve hung beneath her neck and he noticed her smell and the dark brown of her eyes complementing the flowing curves of her soft dark brown hair as she sashayed her hips like one of those catwalk models they used to have back in the day before political correctness saw them replaced by AI animations. She smiled and came up behind him, kissing him gently on the back of the neck and also adjusting his neck tie.

'Wow!' he exclaimed and turned to kiss her once more. He would never get bored of that. Nor would he ever take it for granted again.

'Look at this. I've been using the HIM to find some stuff while I was getting ready.'

He beckoned to the window on the far wall, which did its usual magic dance of first becoming opaque and then displaying the media that was programmed. A series of connected thumbnails appeared, all date coded as if in some sort of chronological order, and after a few prompts from Joe, a specific video appeared on the screen, the background noise coming to both of them from the ceiling above.

'Hahahaha, Daddy. My turn. Run!' A young Benji was sitting on the beach in a mismatched outfit of red shorts, orange T-shirt and a bright white sun hat. He must have been three years old at most.

The camera panned to Joe fake sprinting across the sand as Monica roared with laughter while Benji counted to four, missing out three and then staggered after his dad. The first-person view was compelling, with the sound of the ocean and the bright twilight giving the scene an almost magical feeling. She draped her arms right around Joe's neck and down the front of his dapper ensemble as she kissed him again and simply said, 'Thank you.'

Who was it that said, 'You don't appreciate what you've got until its gone'? Or was it a song?

They were both thinking and feeling about this old mantra, the beautiful memory of the family they had been. And the family they were going to become was the perfect send-off to this happiest of days.

'Come on then, hurry up. Don't want to be late,' she whispered as she turned and left. And Joe couldn't resist a peek at the rear view behind him of the beauty whose value he certainly had now remembered. And then some.

He thought back to that night of the unravelling.

Despite the president's protestations, people did not leave the streets. Nor did they in Paris, or Berlin or

London. Or Bangkok, or Sydney or Singapore. The world over continued over a month of running battles between the mass populace and the Government and the police. Finally, the governmental overreach of the past two decades had been brought to task by an exhausted but emboldened society. Governments were there to serve people, not the other way around.

Snap elections were called all over the planet, and new systems of governance were created, mirroring the work with the AI and Robotics and establishing back the old-fashioned values of the Hippocratic oath at the centre of all things political.

'First, do no harm.'

Centrist political parties sprang up all over the world, neither full Left nor Right, but all of them firmly libertarian, if for sure not Liberal itself by any means. This was now a dirty word like confederate had been at one time in history – like when that country band had been forced to drop 'Dixie' from their name way back in the early 2020's.

Freedom to choose, to vote, to live, to pay fair tax, to keep fair earnings, to help those in need but first incentivise them to help themselves. These factors all came to the fore in the new political world.

The winter had been mild, the storms had stopped, the most ferocious El Niño de Navidad system ever known was now over, and everyone looked forward to a dawn of a new era, one where wealth would be a shared, collective goal. New rules had been brought in regarding singular ownership of corporations, avoiding the distinct two-tier class system that had exploded from the late 1980s right through to the 2030s. Never again would oligarchs rule Russia, or technocrats rule the Western world, infiltrating governments and planting all sorts of nefarious seeds to make them ever richer. Just like the now well understood Covid debacle of the early 2020s, started and created by people with vested interests in the pharmaceutical world, and who stood to gain by recurring infections, masks and lockdowns, and repeated vaccines into arms year upon year.

'First, do no harm.'

It was now more than a long-standing mantra for doctors and physicians. It was how the world lived their lives, how people governed themselves, and how their amazing technology also governed itself to serve all yet protect us all.

China hadn't made landfall in Taiwan, and they had called off their attack just in time for the international community to gather together and discuss the consequences should they have done so. Work was still needed to bring the new 'human first' philosophy to all corners of the world, but hope was strong that humanity was finally uniting under a new way of governance.

'First, do no harm.'

'Come on, let's go,' said Monica as she grasped Joe's hand. 'There are a lot of people waiting to see you, honey, and we are so proud of you.'

Benji appeared at the top of the stairs, a mini version of Joe in morning suit and tails, as handsome as anything she had ever seen. They stood at the top of the stairs, as the HIM gave them final instructions for the car pick-up and the journey's ETA. And they all smiled as the world at the bottom of the stairs was one that had finally unravelled, that had healed. And they had healed with it. Monica took a couple of steps, holding tightly to the handrail, and somewhat instinctively moved her hand to her stomach, which Joe clocked in an instant. Could it be?

As they stepped out towards the car dock, they all held hands and smiled at the sunshine. The ceremony was going to be epic, and Joe was so proud that he'd got his family back together, and he'd helped avert a disaster that could have been global, and for all humanity.

The future was now bright. The future should always be bright.

About the Author

Will Gibson lives in Newcastle with wife, Victoria, and their two children, Elijah and Xanthe.

Gibson is a successful executive in the retail and telecoms space. He has visited over 75 countries and has lived in the UK, Moscow, Singapore, Miami and Athens during his lifetime. An avid traveller and a lover of science fiction from Arthur C. Clarke to namesake William Gibson, it's long been on his bucket list to write a novel. He started in 2018 writing on an iPhone while on yet another international flight.

What Will Gibson says about this book:

In short, I love my story, and I love predicting the near future as it's what I do for my day job in Telecoms. As Head of Sales and Marketing for a software company, I write and present blogs, vlogs, and stage keynotes to over 1,000 people on a regular basis, often thinking about where my industry is heading and predicting the new trends to look out for—some of which are in my book. I think my story could appeal to people who wonder where the world is going.

Milton Keynes UK
Ingram Content Group UK Ltd.
UKHW010648170124
436161UK00002B/5